A Thin Line Between Me and My Thug

Tina J

Warning:

This book is strictly Urban Fiction and the story is **NOT REAL**!

Characters will not behave the way you want them to; nor will they react to situations the way you think they should. Some of them may be drug addicts, kingpins, savages, thugs, rich, poor, ho's, sluts, haters, bitter ex-girlfriends or boyfriends, people from the past and the list can go on and on. That is what Urban Fiction mostly consists of. If this isn't anything you foresee yourself interested in, then do yourself a favor and don't read it because it's only going to piss you off. ☺☺

Also, the book will not end the way you want so please be advised that the outcome will be based solely on my own thoughts and ideas. I hope you enjoy this book that y'all made me write. Thanks so much to my readers, supporters, publisher and fellow authors and authoress for the support. 😮😮

Author Tina J

More books from me:

The Thug I Chose 1, 2 & 3

A Thin Line Between Me and My Thug 1 & 2

I Got Luv For My Shawty 1 & 2

Kharis and Caleb: A Different Kind of Love 1 & 2

Loving You Is A Battle 1 & 2 & 3

Violet and The Connect 1 & 2 & 3

You Complete Me

Love Will Lead You Back

This Thing Called Love

Are We In This Together 1,2 &3

Shawty Down To Ride For a Boss 1, 2 &3

When A Boss Falls in Love 1, 2 & 3

Let Me Be The One 1 & 2

We Got That Forever Love

Aint No Savage Like The One I Got 1&2

A Queen and A Hustla 1, 2 & 3

Thirsty For A Bad Boy 1&2

Hassan and Serena: An Unforgettable Love 1&2

Caught Up Loving A Beast 1, 2 & 3

A Street King And His Shawty 1 & 2

I Fell For The Wrong Bad Boy 1&2

I Wanna Love You 1 & 2

Addicted to Loving a Boss 1, 2, & 3

I Need That Gangsta Love 1&2

Creepin With The Plug 1 & 2

All Eyes On The Crown 1,2&3

When She's Bad, I'm Badder: Jiao and Dreek, A Crazy Love Story 1,2&3

Still Luvin A Beast 1&2

Her Man, His Savage 1 & 2

Marco & Rakia: Not Your Ordinary, Hood Kinda Love 1,2 & 3

Feenin For A Real One 1, 2 & 3

A Kingpin's Dynasty 1, 2 & 3

What Kinda Love Is This: Captivating A Boss 1, 2 & 3

Frankie & Lexi: Luvin A Young Beast 1, 2 & 3

A Dope Boys Seduction 1, 2 & 3

My Brother's Keeper 1. 2 & 3

C'Yani & Meek: A Dangerous Hood Love 1, 2 & 3

When A Savage Falls for A Good Girl 1, 2 & 3

Eva & Deray 1 & 2

Blame It On His Gangsta Luv 1 & 2

Falling for The Wrong Hustla 1, 2 & 3

I Gave My Heart to A Jersey Killa 1, 2 & 3

Luvin The Son of a Savage 1, 2 & 3

A Dopeman and His Shawty 1, 2 & 3

Somebody Else's Thug 1, 2 & 3

Can't Trust Them Thugs 1, 2 &3

Paige

"In the case between Wright vs. Wright, both the plaintiff and defendant have agreed to divide all of their assets. There's no need to draw these divorce proceedings out any longer." The judge said and took his glasses off.

"I have to say that this has been one of the easiest and most civilized divorce cases I have presided over. I wish you both the best of luck. Court Adjourned." I gave my lawyer a hug and grabbed my stuff to leave. I looked at Kamal who was still talking to his lawyer, nodded my head, and walked out with my friend Hope.

"Bitch, we are going out to celebrate your divorce, and I'm not taking no for an answer."

"I don't know Hope. I just wanted to go home, take a bath, with a glass of wine, and chill for the night."

"Oh, hell no. You've been in the house for months, and it's time to get out. I'll be by to pick you up around ten, so be ready and don't take your ass to sleep. I know after eight, you be ready to hit the bed." She said, laughing and getting into her car.

I couldn't believe that after twelve years of marriage, I was finally a free woman. I guess it was cause for a celebration. I drove to the mall to find something to wear and see if the nail salon had any openings.

She was right; I needed a night on the town. It was only right; being as though I had been working like a slave, I really haven't had time for myself. Needless to say, three hours later, I was finally home taking that bath with my glass of wine in my hand.

I reached over to get my phone that started to vibrate. It was a text from Hope.

Hope: *Hey, you better be getting ready.*

Me: *I am girl. I'm about to get out the tub now.*

Hope: *Ok. There's some big party going on, and since my man is the bouncer, we don't have to wait in line.*

Me: *Ok, good, because I didn't really want to sit in line with no ghetto ass chick's anyway.*

Hope: *See you in a few.*

After I hung the phone up, I let all the water out of the tub and turned the shower on. Yes, I liked taking baths, but when I have to shave, I need to turn the shower on. Who wanted all that hair sticking to them from the bath water?

I finished all my hygiene, stepped out and started to get ready. I turned the radio on to that new station 103.9, and they were playing all the old R&B songs. I'm telling you, Tyrese was right when he said that, that type of R&B music needed to come back. Nobody wanted to hear all that booty popping music all the time, and the slow jams today are nowhere near the same.

I grabbed my cucumber melon lotion from Bath and Body Works and rubbed it all over. I put my black laced panties on and admired myself in the mirror. Shit, for me to be thirty-five, I must say that I still had it. I picked up my black bond BCBG leggings, a criss cross halter, my black Bren-Lace-Up pumps, threw on some silver jewelry, because I was not really fond of gold, applied my MAC makeup, and headed out the door.

"Damn, bitch, you trying to catch a man, tonight? That outfit is bad." Hope said as I got in her car.

"Girl, shut up. You aren't looking too bad yourself."

Hope was my best friend from middle school. We had been through everything together, including fights with other bitches, sharing the same man and not knowing, and other shit. She was my ride or die bitch right there. She was quick to cut a bitch if it came down to it, too.

She had on a red razor back dress, leopard pumps, and her make-up was on point. Hope was a beautiful Spanish chick that was about 5'4, very petite, and short hair. She had a big chest and an ass the men loved.

We didn't get to the club until midnight, which was fine with me because I didn't want to be the first chick there anyway. We parked, walked straight to where her man was standing, and went straight in.

Hope was the same age as I, but her man was younger than her by six years. I mean, he was fine and all but I was good dating in my own age range. Ain't nobody have time to be training no niggas. I wanted a man who already knew what to do to my body, without me pointing him to my spots. Shit, I dealt with the same shit for years and I wanted somebody to make my body do things it had never done.

The party was definitely in full effect. It was standing room only when we got there, but we were able to find two seats at the bar. The bartender came over, asked us what we wanted and walked away.

I glanced around the club and noticed there were at least, four or five different VIP areas, a ton of different booths, a lounge area, another bar area, and a big ass dance floor.

"Girl, its some fine ass men in here. I just wish I knew how old they all were." I yelled in Hope's ear because the music was so loud.

"Paige, cut the shit. You had to be over twenty-five to get in, and maybe you need a young, thug type of dude to rock your world. We all know Kamal's old ass only like it in the missionary position." She said cracking up. I almost spit my drink out when she said it. She was right, though.

Kamal and I were high school sweethearts. We went to the same college just to remain together and got married after we graduated. I thought the sex would change once we got married, but I guess once you let someone get comfortable around you, there was no need to change.

I remember the first time he and I had sex; we both decided to wait until we were in college and I was so ready.

I had an apartment, because my parents said staying on campus would be too much of a distraction. I had been stressing over mid-terms and started drinking. Kamal came over just as I was beginning to feel tipsy.

"Hey babe. Come on in." I grabbed him close, pulled his face to mines and kissed him. We began feeling each other up, then I took my shirt off and told him to follow me to the bedroom. I laid back, took the rest of my clothes off, and watched his eyes pop out his head.

"Paige, are you sure you're ready." I figured he was nervous, being as both of us were virgins.

"Yes. I'm ready. Get over here." He took his clothes off while I grabbed a condom out my nightstand. Yes, I bought them for when I was ready. He climbed on top of me, kissed my neck, moved down to my chest, and went down to taste my treasure. I must admit, he did his thing in between my legs. He had me very wet, but it wasn't one of the earth-shaking experiences that I heard women talk about it.

He started rubbing the head of his dick on my pussy;

and it took him a few

minutes to push through my tunnel. But when he did, it fucking hurt like hell. I don't care what nobody says, that shit hurt the entire time.

When we finished, I was bleeding, my pussy was sore, and my drunkenness wore off. He kept apologizing, but it didn't matter, no one could take that pain away. I sent him home, and said we could try it again when I wasn't hurting anymore.

We tried a few more times, before I finally started enjoying it. We did it in every position, and I must say, on top was my favorite. I loved watching my juices flow down his dick.

After we got married, Kamal became uninterested in sex, and I found myself wondering if he was cheating. When I would ask what the problem was, he would just go down on me, then fuck me, but only in the missionary position. If I asked him to go for another round, this nigga would say he was too tired. This shit went on for years, and because I was the devoted wife, I refused to cheat or break up my marriage over it.

Kamal came home one day and said he wanted a divorce, and instead of being mad, I just said, 'Okay, file the paperwork'. I think we both knew it was for the best. Years later, we were finalizing our divorce and I still have yet to experience my first orgasm.

"Paige, let's go. My song is on." Hope said, grabbing my arm and leading me to the dance floor. Chris Brown and Tyga's song, "Ayo", came on and I swear, everybody in the club was dancing and singing that shit.

I felt someone dancing behind me and just assumed it was Hope, but when I turned around, I looked straight into the face of what appeared to be a Greek god.

I felt his hands caressing my body, as we grinded up against one another. This man was at least, six foot, with brown skin. He had waves in his hair, brown eyes, and his swag was on point. He wore a Bathing Ape shirt, with some jeans I couldn't see the label to, a pair of Prada sneakers, and he had diamonds all over. I mean his ear, fingers, arm, around his neck; and anywhere else you could wear them.

We stayed on the dance floor a little longer until some chick grabbed his arm. Hope and I went and found our seats at the bar and ordered more drinks. As we were sitting there, the bartender came back with a bottle of Patron on ice.

"Compliments of the guy you were dancing with." I looked around for him, raised my glass, and mouthed the words *thank you*. When he came to speak to me, Hope jumped up and left. After talking to him for a few minutes, I knew he was about to take me on a roller coaster ride.

Hope

I was so glad my girl finally got her damn divorce over with. I was going to make sure she had some fun since she was single. I was taking her to my man's cousin's birthday party over in Asbury Park, at the Watermark. The only reason that I was taking her was because you had to be twenty-five to get in and she didn't want to mess with any young cats. Shit, I told her that's was what hell she needed to rock her world.

Don't get it twisted, Paige and I are the same age, but my man is six years younger than me and I must say, he puts it down in the bedroom. I wasn't too keen on messing around with someone younger than myself, but fuck it, you only live once; plus, he was very mature.

I met Ezrah last year when I went out to have drinks with some chicks from my job. We were at Fridays on a Sunday during football season, when he and a few of his friends walked in. I noticed him staring at me the entire time he was there. He even sent drinks over to my friends and me. As I was sitting there, I felt some liquid in my panties, which made me run to the restroom.

"I'll be back y'all. I need to use the bathroom." I told the girls I was with. I was so mad when I got inside because I got my period. I came back out having to cut my night short.

"All right ladies. It's time for me to go. I will see y'all at work, tomorrow. Drive

Safe." I told them, as I grabbed my purse to leave. I pressed the alarm on my 2015 Nissan Altima and got in. I'm not trying to buy no expensive ass car and have high ass payments. That shit drove just as nice and cost less.

"Excuse me. Can I talk to you for a minute?" I heard as I sat down in my car.

"Yes. How can I help you?"

"My name is Ezrah, and I was wondering if I can take you out sometimes?"

I looked him over and realized how cute he was. He was tall, with a caramel complexion, muscles everywhere, brown eyes, bowlegged, and he had dreads. Now, I was not usually into dreads or those beards, but I was willing to compromise with him.

We exchanged numbers, and I came to find out he was a fitness trainer, owned two gyms, and did security once in a while. That's why he was at this party; because the guy throwing it was his cousin.

Now here Paige and I were back at the bar, waiting for the bartender to bring our drinks, when he came back and said, "This is for you." It was a bottle of Patron on ice.

"Who is this from?" We both asked at the same time.

"This is courtesy of the guy you were just dancing with. He wanted you to enjoy this on him." The bartender said as we stood there in shock, looking around for the guy.

"Bitch, do you know who the fuck you were dancing with?"

"Girl, hell no! You know, I don't know any of the people in here. How the hell am I going to know who he is?" Just as I was about to tell her, my man walked up.

"Hey, baby. I'm done doing security. I'm going to sit with my cousin for a bit. Let me know when you're ready?" He moved in closer.

"You're coming over so I can tear that shit up, tonight." He said, tonguing me down.

"Hey Paige. Congratulations on your divorce. How does it feel to be single again?"

"It feels real good. Thanks for asking."

"Where did you get this Patron from? I was going to send you that pineapple Ciroc' you like."

"Hmmmm, why don't you ask your cousin? He's the one who sent it to Paige."

"Oh, shit, for real? Paige, what you do? That nigga don't buy any chicks a drink, and here you got the entire bottle. Let me find out." He said, kissing my cheek and walking into VIP.

Paige started looking up to the VIP area where Ezrah went. She lifted her glass, smiled, and mouthed the words *thank you* to the guy who sent the drink.

"Anyway, bitch. That's Hakim, Ezrah's cousin. That nigga is paid out the ass, and if he's buying you a drink, it means he's interested."

"I'm good, Hope. I just got divorced a few hours ago. I'm not trying to jump into anything; plus, he has a ton of women up there dying for his attention. Let's finish this Patron and be out. It's already three in the morning."

"Ok, I'm going to send Ezrah a text to tell him we're leaving." We finished up the bottle, and stood up to leave, when I saw Hakim walking in our direction.

"Oh shit, girl. Don't look now, but he's on his way down here, so get ready."

I could tell she was nervous. She only had one man in her life, and he was now a non-factor.

"What's up, Hope? Who's your friend right here?" He asked, kissing me on the cheek.

"Hakim, this is Paige. Paige, this is Hakim, and I'm gone." I left her ass sitting right there, while I went up to my man. I sat on his lap and watched them talk. I didn't need to hear what he was saying, because she would tell me word-for-word tomorrow.

Hakim

Today, I was having a party over at the Watermark bar, in Asbury, and was hoping that no shit kicked off. I called up my cousin, Ezrah, to see if he could be one of my security guys working the door. The club offered security, but shit, my little sister could probably beat them, so I hired some of my own people that weren't going to be scared of the ignorant ass people that showed up.

I went to the barbershop that morning and ran straight into Noel. I didn't want to get out of my car to deal with her ass, but I knew that that day would come, so I might as well had gotten it over with.

"What's up, Noel? How you been?" She rolled her eyes.

"What do you mean what's up? You tell me it's over, then come over last week to fuck me, and I haven't heard from you since. I've been calling and texting you. What's up with that?"

I was now sitting on the hood of my car, rolling a blunt, listening to her go on and on. That was what I hated about chicks; when you told them it was over, they didn't get it. Yes, maybe I shouldn't have fucked her after I broke it off, but she could've said no.

"Listen, Noel, before you start that shit. You didn't have to fuck me, so don't come to me with that. Second, we have been together for, what, six years, and this ain't what it used to be." I said, pointing from her to me. "You know we been rocky ever since you cheated. I thought I could get past that, but I guess I couldn't. So, instead, of trying to make it work; this is probably best. I won't fuck you anymore."

"Are you serious right now, Hakim? It was one time, and I was drunk."

"You're right. It was one time, and you were drunk, but guess what? That nigga taped your ass. What do you expect me to do when he has my woman on video fucking and sucking? I can't believe you even went down on that nigga, as if he was your man."

"I didn't even enjoy it, Hakim."

"Shit, it looks like you enjoyed it to me, and I'm sure any and every one else would say the same thing that watched it. Noel, we'll always have the six years, but this relationship has run its course. You have to find someone to make you happy, because it's obvious that I didn't."

Here comes the waterworks, I thought to myself. I took a pull from my blunt and waited.

"Do you even love me, anymore?"

"Noel, I will always love you. You were my first love, but when it's over, it's over. If you want to know if I shed a tear over you? Absolutely, I don't have anything to be ashamed of. Niggas cry too. But you know, I don't do this public arguing shit, and you're out here making a spectacle of yourself, once again."

"Hakim, I took you back after all the cheating you did. How can you not do the same for me?"

"Ok, Noel, you did. But, it's different when a man cheats than when a woman does it. I probably would have taken you back had there not been a video, but I can't. Out of all the women I cheated with, none of them can tell you that I went down on her or even kissed her. That shit is too intimate and personal. My woman is the only one that can get that, but you gave it up like it didn't mean anything." That shit was pissing me off just thinking about it. I kissed her on the cheek and said, "I have to go, now. I'll see you around." I told her, throwing my blunt to the ground.

I watched her walk to the car, crying, and pull off. Noel was my first love, and yes, I cheated on her quite a few times, and she took me back, but when you see your woman on video fucking some dude and giving him head, that was something that wouldn't go away. It was fucked up, because I really was going to make her my wife, but I was glad that I found out sooner than later how she was.

Now, here I was, sitting at my party hours later, enjoying myself, with so many different choices of women to take home. I'm saying; it was my birthday, and it was only right for me to have a treat. I sat up in VIP looking around, when I saw this chick with my cousin's girlfriend, Hope. She was light-skinned, with long hair, that you could tell was hers; she had to be, at least, a size twelve with all those hips. Her ass wasn't as big as I was used to, but that was ok. She had on an all-black outfit that showed off the curves she did have.

Now, if she was with Hope, she had to be in her thirty's, at least, because that was how old she was. I put the drink down I had, walked down the steps, grabbed her hips, and started dancing with her. Shorty was bad up close. She looked at me and had the prettiest smile; a little bit of freckles and the way she moved her body to the music had me mesmerized. I was about to talk to her when Noel's ass grabbed my arm, yelling about me not wanting her. I had to get her ass removed, because she was causing a scene with her nonsense.

When I went back to dance, shorty was gone. I spotted her at the bar and sent a bottle of Patron to her. My cousin told me that they were getting ready to leave, so I went down there to introduce myself.

"Hello, my name is Hakim. What's your name?"

"Hi, Hakim. My name is Paige. And, thank you for the drink. Next time, I'm a Ciroc kind of woman."

"Ok, love. What are you doing when you leave her?"

"I'm going home, and what about you? Wait, before this conversation goes any further, how old are you?"

"I'm twenty-eight. Why does it matter how old I am?"

"You're just a baby to me."

"How old are you?"

"You're never supposed to ask a woman her age. But, I just turned thirty-five, if you must know."

"Ok. That's all the more reason why I want to get to know you. Am I younger than you? Yes. But a baby, I'm not. Trust me. I will show you some things and have you speaking in tongues before it's all said and done."

I could tell that I had just made her cum all in her pants, just by the way she looked and crossed her legs.

"Let me get your number, and we can go from there. You know what, let me get your phone. I'm going to program my number in your phone, and you decide when you think I'm old enough." She handed me her phone, and I saved it.

"I'll be waiting for you to call." I whispered in her ear.

I kissed her cheek and went back upstairs. I sat down, watching her fan herself. She must've texted Hope, because she looked down at her phone, got off my cousin's lap, and went back over there. I could see Hope asking her what had happened, and the smile that spread across her face showed me that I got to her ass. They grabbed their stuff, she looked up, smirked, and left. I knew it was a matter of time before she called.

Ezrah

When I woke up this morning, Hope was already gone. She had to go with her friend, Paige, to the courthouse so that she could finalize her divorce. Marriage just ain't what it used to be. How do you stay married for so many years, then one day, just up and say you're done? I guess to each his own. I picked my phone up and saw I had a few messages.

Hope: *Hey, Baby. I didn't want to wake you, but I made you breakfast. It's in the microwave when you're ready to eat. I'll see you, tonight.*

Hakim: *What's up? Don't forget to be at the club around nine, but my moms wants you to come by. She didn't tell me why, so I guess you'll find out when you get here. One.*

Ashley: *Hey boss. Before you come in, can you stop by Dunkin Donuts and pick up some munchkins. We have quite a bit of kids here today for some reason.*

I responded to all the messages and went to the kitchen to eat. Hope made me some eggs, bacon, and potatoes. I heated the food up, poured me a glass of orange juice, and sat at the table to eat. I met Hope last year at Fridays. I didn't think she wanted to mess with me, because I was younger than her, but she proved me wrong. She and I hit it off right from the start. We went out on dates, to clubs, and she taught me just how to love her.

See, we as men thought that we knew what a woman wanted, but that was not always true. Most men didn't realize that, when you go down on a woman, she is showing you what she wants. You'll hear her when she says, 'right there', or when she moves her pussy around in your mouth trying to get you to touch that spot, she is letting you know what works for her.

I'm not saying that I couldn't please her; I'm just saying that she showed me the way that she wanted to be pleased, and now, she doesn't have to open her mouth, because it's already done. Every woman wants something different, but you, as a man, have to take your time to learn just as she will do the same with you. Now, Ashley, the woman that works at one of my gyms, could care less how she gets fucked. I know that's unprofessional of me, but that kind of just happened.

One day, I was sitting in my office, and she came in, crying, about how her boyfriend cheated on her with some chick. I was sitting on the edge of my desk, listening, when I reached over to get her some tissue; she got up and stood face to face with me. She moved in to kiss me, and I backed up.

"Ashley, You're upset, and I think it's best for you to leave."

"I don't want to leave, and I don't think you want me to,

either." She said, while

she was rubbing my dick through my pants. I pushed her hand away and stood up. I was sure that she could see my man standing at attention.

"That's enough, Ashley, I want you to leave."

Before I could say another word, her tongue was down my throat, and her hand was inside my pants. She pulled my pants and boxers down and put my man in her mouth. I know I should've stopped her, but fuck it; it was too late now. That line was crossed between boss and employee, and there was no turning back.

Once I released all my seeds down her throat, I bent that ass over my desk and fucked the shit out of her. She was screaming like I was killing her, and I didn't care, because the gym was closed, and we were the only ones there.

Ashley and I continued to fuck almost every day, since that night, until I met Hope. That shit was a wrap when she came into my life. Unfortunately, Ashley wasn't trying to hear that shit. I didn't come to work, now, unless I knew that other employees were going to be there. I knew that I shouldn't have been scared to go into my own place of business, but I didn't have time for no sexual harassment lawsuits. That was why, when I broke that shit off with her, I recorded her ass.

"Ashley, this can no longer continue. I have a woman now, and what we had was

just a fling. No more, no less."

"Come on, Ezrah. I know you miss me and the way I can make you cum." I had to adjust my dick, because it was swelling up just hearing her speak about what she can do with her mouth.

"Ashley, this is over. I can move you to the other gym that I'm barely at, so we don't have to be around one another, if that's what you want."

"No, this is not over, and I'm staying right here." That bitch started yelling and shit; I had to get security to escort her ass out of here. I told Hope about her ass, and of course, she wanted to come in and whoop her ass. I did have her come in a few times, just so Ashley could meet her. She seemed to have calmed down a lot after she met Hope; she knew that she was no joke. Every now and then, she would ask me if we were still together and try some shit, but I was good. I didn't need any stalkers in my life.

Hope and I are in a good space, and I was even thinking about asking her to move in with me. Shit, we together at each other's spot every night, anyway, so why have two places. I finished eating, got dressed, and went on about my day. I went home a little early so that I could rest up for my cousin's party later, because I knew that it would be an all night thing, and I had to make sure I had enough rest to deal with the bullshit.

The party went pretty well, besides me having to throw Noel's ass out for causing a damn scene over Hakim. I walked up to Hope and saw that they had a bottle of Patron in front of them. When she told me my cousin bought it, I was shocked, as hell. He never brought chick's a drink. He always said, "Woman think they're slick when they come into a bar. They spend all their money on outfits, then come into the bar trying to get free drinks." The only person he bought drinks for was his ex, Noel, and her friends, but that's about it.

I made a bet with Hope that he wouldn't be able to get Paige to give him the time of day, because she was too stuck on the whole age thing; she said that anyone under thirty was too young for her. We looked at Hakim whisper in Paige's ear, and it must've made her feel some kind of way, because she smiled and shifted in her seat. Hope and I just laughed when we saw him program his information in her phone. Hope went to take her home and said that she would be back at my house in an hour.

"Yo, what did you say to her? She was smiling hard as hell." I asked my cousin, as he stared down to Paige. She looked up, smirked at his ass and left.

"Just know that I gave her ass something to think about, and I bet she goes home tonight fantasizing about a nigga." I had a few drinks with him, wished him a Happy Birthday, and headed out.

When I got home, Hope had just stepped out the shower. I grabbed her by the waist and placed kisses down the back of her neck. She unwrapped her towel, letting it fall to the floor. Hope gasped when I took my thumb, circled her clit with it, then played in her wetness; listening to her moan had me rock hard. She got tired of me teasing her, laid on the bed with her legs wide open, and told me to come get it.

I took my tongue and licked her pearl, slowly, up, down, and every which way possible. She had her hand on the back of my head, while she continued to fuck my face. I felt her pearl getting harder, so I looked at her while she burst in my mouth like one of those candies with the cream in the middle. I kept licking, giving her multiple orgasms. I tried to give her time to catch a breath, but I needed to feel her. I grabbed a condom, put her legs on my shoulder, and dug deep into her pussy.

"Oh my god, Ezrah, it feels so good. Don't stop."

"You like this young dick, don't you?" I asked, while I was fucking her brains out.

"No, I love this young dick. Fuck, baby, I'm going to cum, again." I had her turn over, and I rammed my dick back inside over and over. The sounds of our lovemaking and her moaning had a nigga going crazy.

"Yea, Hope, throw it back like that. Just like that." I said, smacking her ass. "I'm about to cum, Hope. You know what I want you to do."

She turned around, snatched the condom off, and put him in her mouth. I loved the way she looked up at me, as she sucked the life out of me. She glided her hands up and down my dick getting every baby out. I was done, but she wanted more, so we had sex for the rest of the night or what was left of

it.

Paige

After Hope dropped me off, I couldn't get that young dude off my mind. The shit he whispered in my ear had my panties wet. I don't think a man had ever spoken to me like that and it have such an effect on me. That shit had me scrolling through my phone looking for his number.

Should I call him? Wait, what if he has a woman? Nah, he couldn't by the way he was talking. Maybe, I'll call him and see if he can come show me tonight. No, it's too quick, I just met him. Fuck it, I'll call him tomorrow. I'm not sure if I want to mess with him, anyway. It's probably the liquor making me feel this way, so I'm just going to take my ass to bed and see if I feel the same when I get up.

"Paige, get your ass up. It's two o' clock." Hope said, sitting on the edge of my bed.

"Hope, what are you doing here? I just knew you and Ezrah would be up all night fucking, and I wouldn't hear from you until tonight."

"Bitch, you already know we were. Anyway, I figured we could go out to eat since Ezrah was meeting up with Hakim. Oh yea, what that nigga say to you last night that had you smiling like that?" I got out the bed to use the bathroom, and she followed behind.

"Damn, let me pee first."

"Bitch, please. I've seen you piss, shit, and dress; ain't no need to hide now. Tell me what he said."

"All right." I wiped my ass, washed my hands, and went into the room to find something to wear.

"He, basically, told me that he wasn't young, that he will make my body do things it' had never done, and that he would have me speaking in tongues, when it's all said and done."

"Dammmmmnnn, girl. Shit, I probably would've came in my drawers, too. So, what are you going to do?" She asked, texting on her phone.

"Hope, I don't know. This nigga got up in my head with what he said; he had me wanting to call him up after I got home to show me."

We both burst out laughing hard, as hell. I jumped in the shower, threw on some denim skinny jeans, with the rips on the knees, an orange cowl neck top that drapes down in the middle, and my orange wedges. I fixed my hair, picked up my keys, phone, and purse and left. We pulled up at this place, called McCloones, that was located on the beach.

The waitress put us at a table, by the window, overlooking the beach. She took our drink orders and said she that would be back to take our food orders.

"Hope, this is nice. How did you find this place?"

"I asked her to bring you here." I heard from behind. I looked up, and it was Hakim and Ezrah. I felt my pussy throb, instantly, as he pulled a chair up next to me. He had on all black, and that shit looked sexy as fuck on him.

I looked at Hope, who acted like she was looking at the menu, so I kicked her ass under the table. When she looked up, she was smiling, which let me know she was in on that shit. When the waitress came back, she noticed them and took their drink orders before walking away.

"Good morning, beautiful." He sai,d making me blush.

"Good morning, Hakim. How are you today?" I asked him, looking down at the menu. I didn't know what to do or feel at that moment. Kamal was the only man I had ever been on a date with or even been intimate with.

"Did you think about what I told you last night?" He whispered in my ear, so they couldn't hear. Oh my God, this man smelled so good and had me dripping wet.

"Yes, I did." Was all I could say? My words were stuck in my throat." He smiled, and I couldn't sit there any longer.

"Excuse me. I need to go to the ladies room."

He stood up, and whispered, "Make sure you clean her up well. I can't wait until you let me taste you."

My face had to be beet red by then. That nigga had my body going through something, and he hadn't even touched me.

"What the fuck is going on?" I asked Hope. She was laughing her ass off, as I grabbed some paper towels and put some water on them. I went into the stall and wiped myself, because I couldn't do anything but laugh.

"Bitch, let me find out this nigga had you cumming on yourself."

"Fuck you, bitch. And, why didn't you tell me he was coming?"

"I knew you would say no if I told you. Relax, Paige. I know this is all knew to you, but you have to try to calm down. I can tell he got you feeling some kind of way, so maybe you should see what he's talking about."

"Fuck, I don't know how much longer I can sit out there with him without wanting to take him home."

"So what if you take him home. We are all grown. Aint nobody going to judge you. Let's go back in there before they send a search party for us."

"Yea, I guess, but he's not coming home with me. Yet."

"Ok, girl. Oh, did you make sure you cleaned up well?"

"Fuck you, Hope." I pushed her ass out the bathroom door.

When we got back to the table, he and Ezrah were talking about something. He stood up to let me get back to my chair, but not before talking more shit.

"I told you I would have your body doing some things. Don't worry, when you give me your body, it will feel better."

I guess I should've never said he was a baby, because the shit he was saying was proving me wrong. The waitress came back and took our food orders. We stayed at the restaurant for about two hours, talking and laughing. Hakim told Hope that he would give me a ride home, because he wanted to get to know me. We went to his car, which was a 2015 Cadillac Escalade/ESV. I admired the truck on the way to my house. I wasn't sure if I should've invited him in, but it was only right being that he gave me a ride home.

I dropped my keys on the kitchen table, got a bottle of water, and sat on the couch with him. I turned the TV on, placed my water on the coffee table, and started to speak.

"Why are you staring at me?"

"I'm just looking at how beautiful you are. And, I like your freckles." I put my head down, smiling.

He leaned in closer and parted my lips with his tongue. His lips were so soft and his kiss was gentle. That feeling between my legs had me wanting to get naked right then. I pushed him back trying to catch my breath.

"I'm sorry, Hakim. I think we're moving to fast." I said, jumping off the couch.

"Come here." He said, pulling me down to him on the couch. I sat on his lap and let him grind his dick against my pussy. Even though we were fully dressed, I could feel his dick trying to break free.

"We don't have to do anything you don't want to. I know you think it's too quick, but we're grown, and if it's meant to happen, just let it." He said, placing kisses all over my neck. He went to put his hand up my shirt, but his phone started ringing. Whew! I was saved by his phone. I got up off him, but he grabbed my hand. Whoever was on the phone had his full attention.

"I'll be right there." He said, hanging the phone up.

"Paige, I'm really feeling you, and you can't deny this sexual attraction we have towards one another. Is it ok if I stop by later?"

"I guess, if that's what you want to do."

"Yes, I definitely do. I'll be back around nine. Is that ok?" When I nodded my head, he gave me another one of those kisses and left. I didn't know what that man was doing to me, but I liked it. I went to my room and laid back down to take a nap; I would call Hope later.

Hakim

After meeting Paige last night, she stayed on my mind. I got up this morning and asked my cousin to get his girl to meet us so that I could talk to her again. I knew that I had her feeling me when she left the club, but I wanted to make sure she didn't forget about me. She was shocked when she saw me at the restaurant.

I asked her if she remembered what I told her the night before, and that had her ass running to the bathroom. Even though she was a woman, she still had those needs that I knew I could fulfill. Yea, Hope did a lot of pillow talking with my cousin, so when they went to the bathroom, he told me all about the ex husband who wasn't hitting it right. I was shocked, as hell, when he told me she had never had an orgasm, especially at her age. I was about to turn her ass out, and she didn't even know it.

We ended up enjoying ourselves at lunch; I offered to give her a ride home so that I could talk to her some more. When we walked into her house, I was happy to see that she was a clean woman. She had good taste, as well, which was a plus, because some chicks don't give a fuck what their house look like; they just wanted to look good.

I couldn't resist her when she sat next to me, so I pulled her close and kissed her, but she felt that we were rushing, and she jumped up. I pulled her down on my lap, and my dick tried to bust out of my jeans. My phone interrupted what was about to go down, and I could see the relief on her face. I left to go handle some business, but I was definitely going back that night.

I pulled up at her house around 9:30, put the alarm on my car, and rang her doorbell. I was still on the phone when she opened her door, and she had on a Victoria Secret nightgown that hung off her shoulders and some shorts on underneath. I ended my call and stepped in, kissing her on the lips.

"Hello to you, too. I'll be right back. Let me grab my phone." She said, walking back to her room.

She came back, sat next to me, and turned a movie on. The movie was really watching us, because we talked throughout the entire thing.

"So, what are you getting into for the rest of the night?"

"Nothing much. I told everybody I was going out of town. I shut my phone off, so we wouldn't be interrupted, like earlier. It's all about you, Paige? What do you want to do for the rest of the night? I asked, rolling a blunt.

She stood up, grabbed my hand, and led me to her room. When we got there, she turned around, threw her hands around my neck, and stuck her tongue in my mouth. I pulled away from her to ask if she was sure, and once she said yes, that was it. I placed her on the bed and began to undress her. She scooted back and took her finger to gesture for me to come to her. That shit was sexy, as hell. I got on top of her, kissing her neck and moved down to her breast, taking them in my mouth, one at a time. I flickered back and forth over each nipple, then I moved down to her navel and sucked on her sides and inner thighs, right before I got to her middle.

I opened her legs, took my fingers to open the slit of her pussy, and saw that she had already started flowing. I placed my thick tongue on her lips before taking her clit in my mouth. Her body started to shake, causing her to jump back. I guess she didn't know what was happening to her body.

"Hakim, why is my body shaking like that? What did you do?" I got up and slid my tongue in her mouth, trying to relax her.

"Don't worry, baby. It's called an orgasm. When you feel it coming, just let it go." I told her, going back down to finish feasting.

I stuck two of my fingers inside of her, finding her g spot. I had her pearl swollen in a matter of seconds; then, her body started shaking again. I grabbed her legs so that she couldn't move, because I wanted her to experience the feeling that she had been missing out on for so many years.

"Oh, my god, Hakim. What's happening? Yes, Yes, Yesssssssssss…" She screamed out, while all her juices escaped like a waterfall. She tried to stop me, but I kept going, giving her, yet, another one. I slid up on the bed and told her to sit on my face. She was nervous, at first, but once my tongue lapped over her clit again, she got over that shit.

"Damn, girl, your pussy tastes good, as hell. Don't hold back. I want you to cum in my mouth."

"Shit, Hakim. Are you sure?'

"Yes, let it all out." I said.

"Fuck yea. Oh, shit yea. Suck my pussy just like that. Oh, god, here I cummmmmmmmmm…" She screamed out, falling back on the bed, trying to catch her breath.

I pulled her to the edge and put the head of my dick in her pussy, and she grabbed both of her legs and held them open. I slid him in and noticed that she tensed up a little, but once she got used to it, she started grinding her hips. All you could hear was the swishing noises from our lovemaking. Her pussy started making those farting noises, and she put her legs down.

"Paige, it's ok. You're pussy is so wet. It's supposed to make that noise."

I put her legs down and had her turn around. I entered her from the back and grabbed some of her hair pulling her head back. She turned around, kissing me, before she started moaning and cumming, again. She squirted all over my dick and my stomach. She wanted to get on top, so we switched positions. She stood on her feet, parted her lips to open, and slid down on it. She went up and down, bouncing on it fast, then, and slow. I was going to grab her hips and guide her, but she didn't need any help. She was riding my dick so good, I could barely move myself.

"Paige, you riding the shit out of my dick. I'm about to cum. I want you to cum with me." She leaned back, as I rubbed my fingers over her clit. The harder it got, the faster she rode.

"Hakim, oh, I'm cumming. Yes, Yessssss." She was screaming out again. I was sure the neighbors definitely knew my name by then.

"Fuck, girl, ride that shit. Just like that. Fuckkkkkk… Damn, you got some good ass pussy. Where the fuck you been hiding at?" I asked, as she laid her head on my chest.

Neither one of us wanted to move after that. My dick was still inside of her, so she lifted up to let him slide out.

She kissed my stomach, and then wrapped her mouth around my dick. She took my balls in her mouth, sucking each one, slowly. She used her hands to stroke him at the same time that she sucked. I sat on my elbows, watching, until I couldn't take it anymore. I felt my man stiffening up, as she picked up her speed. I grabbed her head, as I felt my nut coming to the tip, right before she let all my seeds rush down her throat.

"Yo', what the fuck? Your head game is on point. You had a nigga cumming in two minutes." She just smiled and walked in the bathroom. I stepped in behind her and saw that she was brushing her teeth and rinsing her mouth out.

"Why you doing all that?"

"I didn't want to kiss you after I just let you nut in my mouth." I just laughed and kissed her neck; she really had no clue.

"Let's take a shower, together?" I turned the shower on and waited for her to step in. We fucked in her shower, living room, the extra bedroom, and on the kitchen floor. It was like she wanted to Christen her house with me, and I didn't object at all. This woman was the energizer bunny when it came to fucking, or maybe she was making up for all the lost time. We stayed in bed together until the next afternoon.

I had to get back out to handle business, but she had me so drained that I didn't know how long I would be out. I was getting some more of that and, who knew, I may make her my woman. One thing was for sure, I didn't want anyone else up in that pussy but me.

Kamal

It had been two days since I left the courthouse, and I missed the hell out of Paige, but I knew that leaving was best for the both of us. All the nights that I heard her crying to her friend, Hope, about me not loving her or even making love to her like I used to finally got to me. I knew that things had changed between us, but I just didn't know how to make it right. The truth was that I loved having sex with Paige, but I just wasn't into all that switching positions crap. Once I came, I was finished, and would fall straight to sleep. Working sixty hours a week, had me exhausted; I was lucky just to get a few hours of sleep a night. I still remember listening to that phone call.

"Paige, I'm home, baby." I pushed the door open in the bedroom, but her back was turned.

"I tried to get him to change positions or even to go down and please him, but he

just doesn't want to be bothered. It's like he's only fucking me to get his nut, and that's all he cares about."

I closed the door back and went to the bar to have a

drink. I was so hurt that she

felt that way, but she was right, I didn't allow her to express herself, sexually, with me, nor did I with her. When I got back home, she was asleep, so I slept in the other room, because I didn't want to bother her.

After the first time I slept in the extra room, it went

from one day to two days, to

two years. It was like we lived as roommates, instead of, husband and wife. We had sex, maybe, twice in the last few years, and that was when I knew it was over.

I came home from work one day and told her that I was filing for a divorce, and she didn't even fight it.

I rode by her house last night, but didn't knock on the door. I saw a Cadillac truck in front of her house, and I didn't want to disturb her, so since it was Friday, and I had nothing to so. I got home, looked around my house, and cried. This house was full of memories; I was thinking that it was about time to sell it. Of course, everything had to be divided, so whatever I got, she would get half, which was fine, since both of our names were on the mortgage. Let me send her a text.

Me: *Hey, Paige. I wanted to know if you're free one day this week. I wanted to take you to lunch and talk to you about some things.* I waited a few minutes for her to text back.

My wife: *Sure, Kamal. Is Friday a good day?*

Me: *Yes, that's good. Do you want to meet at your favorite spot?*

Paige: *You know it.*

Me: *Ok. Red lobster it is. Friday around 12.*

Paige: *Ok. I'll see you there.*

Well, I may as well go to Home Depot to pick some boxes up and start packing. If I start now, it won't be so much to do when I leave. I sure was going to miss that place, but it was not the same without Paige in it.

Hope

"Bitch, where you been all day?" I yelled into the phone. I had been calling Paige's ass since last night, and when she didn't answer, I rode by. I saw that Hakim's truck was there, so I didn't say shit, but then, her phone was off all day. It was, well after, two o clock when she decided to turn that shit back on. I know she fucked him, and I had to hear the details from miss I don't want no young ass thug in my bed.

"Hello to you too, Hope. I've been home all day."

"Are you home, now?"

"Yea, I'm here."

"Bitch, I'll be right there. Get dressed. Your mom made a Sunday dinner, and I'm not missing that shit.

Ezrah called me on the ride over to Paige's house to tell me that he was watching the game at his aunt's house and that, if I wanted to see him, to come there, or he would see me when he got home. That man, or should I say, young man, had my ass wide open for him. I guess it was true when they said that you can't help who you fall in love with. That is, of course if you're a nasty ass pedophile then you deserve to die.

I got to Paige's door, and went to open it, but the screen was locked, so I had to ring the doorbell. I noticed that her house smelled like cleaning supplies, and when I walked to the back, there were no sheets on her bed. I heard the washer going, so I stood against the wall and stared at her.

"What?"

"You nasty bitch. You fucked him, didn't you?" She knew her ass was caught, because she couldn't even speak. She just smiled and took the mop out the bucket.

"Ugh, hell no. You're not about to mop this floor and act like nothing happened. Put that shit down, and give me details. Well, not all the details."

I grabbed us two beers out the fridge, cracked them open, and took a seat on the porch with her. She began to tell me how he came over after they went out to eat. Then, he came back, but when she said she received her first orgasm, I was so happy for her.

"Hope, you did not tell me that shit will drain your entire body."

"Shit, girl, I can't explain everything to you. You had to experience it for yourself. And, look, a young thug nigga brought that shit out of you. I guess all that shit about being over thirty to fuck with you went straight out the window, huh?"

"Hell, yea, it did. I didn't have to show him shit. Girl, he had me climbing the walls in here. The crazy thing about it was that he really did have my body doing things I didn't know it could. The speaking in tongues part was just an icing on the cake from all the screaming he had me doing. I'm not even going to sugar coat that. I'm surprised the neighbors didn't call the cops from all that yelling I was doing. Then, we had sex all throughout this house. I mean, his dick rose for the occasion every time, like he was on Viagra or something."

"Ok, that sounds all good, but all I want to know is did you throw it on his ass?"

"Hope, you know I can't answer that. I wouldn't even know how to do that. Kamal had me missing out on so many things, sexually, and Hakim did it in one night; well, today, too."

"Ok, let me see how to word this. Did he tell you it was good? Was he saying anything while y'all were fucking?"

"Well, yea. He wasn't screaming out my name, but he was definitely moaning and saying some other shit. I guess, I'll know if we fuck again. Maybe, I'll just ask him."

"Girl, you stupid. Come on, I'll help you finish cleaning, so we can get some of your mom's cooking."

"Hope, don't say anything about Hakim. I don't want anyone to start asking questions, because as of right now, he is just my fuck buddy."

"Don't worry, girl. I got you. Plus, your mom is too worried about asking me a million questions about Ezrah. You know, ever since she met him, she's trying to get us married. Ezrah loves going over there, though, and I swear, he'll stop by there without me. I had to tell that nigga that that aint even my mom's house, but he don't care. Anyway, you know I'm going to find out what's up with Hakim, because him and Ezrah are tight as hell. Oh, shit, there goes Ezrah now.

"Hey, what's up?"

"Don't forget to tell Paige's mom to make me a plate. And, make sure you make your own. I'm tired of you eating off my plate when you could've gotten your own."

"I know, Ez. I promise, I'll get you a plate."

"Alright, I'm pulling up on the block, now, with Hakim."

"Ok, tell him I said what up?"

"He said what up. All right, babe, I'll talk to you later. I love you."

"I love you, too, Ez, and be safe out there."

"Always. I have to make it back to you."

"Really, with all that lovey dovey shit? I mean, shit, y'all just left each other."

I smacked Paige in the arm and followed her inside to clean. Once we were done, we jumped in my car and headed to her mom's house. My mom lived in Connecticut, and I only visited her when it was necessary. My mom was what you called, a hoarder. She was not as bad as the people on TV, though. She hoarded, food, people, cars, and anything. You name it, she had it. The last time I went to her house, she rented out the basement to some Mexican Americans with, like, five kids. There were about five or six broken down cars in her driveway, the yard was a mess, newspapers flooded the living room, her pantry was overflowing with canned foods, and the house was in need of a good cleaning.

The day I took Ez up there to meet her, I kept telling him to please excuse my mom's house. I told him that she was a hoarder, but I think he thought that I was exaggerating. When we got there, his face turned up, and I knew he thought that I didn't see it, but I did. I could see the disgust in his face when we walked inside. I told him to take a seat, but he insisted on standing. I laughed my ass off on the inside, but I couldn't show him, because he would've, probably, get mad.

"Hey, Ma. This is my man, Ezrah. We been together, now, for about nine months. I wanted you two to meet, so here we are."

"Nice to meet you, Ms. Miller." She yanked his arm, when he tried to shake it so that she could hug him. It caught him by surprise, but he hugged her back. That night was one to

remember, as the kids from the basement were running all over the place; they were drinking Coronas in the backyard, and my dad sat his fat ass right on the recliner the whole time, watching TV. He only got up to use the bathroom or to go lay down.

It was getting late, and my mom wanted us to stay, but Ez told her he had to be up early for work and that he was driving home. My mom said that she understood, but I knew he just didn't want to stay there. Ez stood in front of me at the car and put his face in my neck. He whispered in my ear, "Baby, I don't ever want to come back here if we don't have to." I almost peed on myself, because I was laughing so hard. I punched him in the arm, as he held the door open for me to get in the car. We drove home talking about my mom's house. I knew that I probably shouldn't have, but fuck it, we all have trifling family members and mines happened to be my mom. I still loved her; I just couldn't be around her too long.

Paige

Hakim and I had sex all night, and I could say that he blew my mind. I didn't think someone younger then me could do anything for me, but he changed my mind on that. When I woke up the next morning, I thought he had left, but he was in the kitchen making me breakfast. I felt like Nia Long in Love Jones after she threw it on Larenz Tate. I jumped in the shower, while he cooked, wrapped my towel around me, and stepped into my room to find him sitting there waiting for me.

"Good morning, sexy." I said, looking at him smiling.

"Will you look at that? I made you blush this time." He just smiled at me when I said that.

"Good Morning to you, too. Do you have an extra toothbrush, and do you mind if I take a shower? I brought some clothes that I had from my truck in."

"There's extra toothbrushes in my linen closet. And, what makes you think I want you getting dressed when you get out." I ate a piece of bacon, while I waited for him to respond.

“Hold that thought.” He said. I heard him brushing his teeth. The sink cut off, and he came back in the room, moved my food off my lap, and said that I was his breakfast.

“Turn over.”

I got on all fours, waiting for him to enter, so you can imagine how surprised I was when I felt his tongue sliding up and down from my ass to my pussy. He spread my cheeks and dove in like it was a pie-eating contest. My body shook for what felt like ten minutes from the orgasm he gave me. That man’s pussy eating skills should’ve went into the Guinness Book of World Records. We had sex for the rest of the morning and part of the afternoon.

I guess he had stuff to do, and I was ok with that. I had made plans to stop by my mom’s, anyway, and I was not taking him. That was just a fuck thing, and there was no need in introducing them. We showered together and washed each other up. I didn’t know why, but he made it so easy to be comfortable around him. Kamal and I, maybe, took a few showers, together, and there it was, me and Hakim had already took two in one day. I walked him to the door to leave.

"I'll talk to you, later." I told him.

"Ok. Oh, I don't have your number. Can I have it?"

I let him unlock his phone so that I could store my number in it. He kissed me on the lips and left. I was doing my Sunday cleaning when Hope called, yelling. Then, she came over, so that I could tell her what had happened, and she was so happy for me. I just didn't know where Hakim and I would go from there, but oh well. At least, I got to finally experience an orgasm.

Hope and I drove over to my mom's house, and my brother and my annoying ass sister were all outside with a bunch of people. My mom had three kids. I was the oldest. Then, it was my brother Eric, and the baby, Janae. My youngest sister was sixteen and fast, as hell. I felt like she had been fucking since she was twelve, but hey, that was my mom and dad's shit to deal with.

"What's up, everybody? Hope and I yelled out.

My brother, Eric, was standing out there with his best friend, Mark. Mark had been hitting on me since we were kids. He was very handsome, but he had a baby mother from hell, and no one had time for that shit. He was six-feet tall, Dominican, hazel eyes, and he had gaps in his teeth, but you wouldn't know, because of the gold crown at the top and bottom. The crown, definitely, complimented him in a good way. The only thing, besides his baby mama, was that he was in the streets with my brother. I didn't want to deal with no thugs, and Mark knew that. He couldn't leave the streets alone, and I was okay with that, because I wasn't trying to change anyone. We all still hung out every day, until Paige and I went away to college.

"Paige, is that you?" My mom said, coming out on the porch and reaching out to give me a hug.

"Ma, I just saw you last Sunday."

"I know, but I see all my kids every day, except you. I know you work, but you can get over here, at least, one day out of the week." She said, before walking into the house.

"Hope, get your ass in here and make your man a plate. And, he better not call me and say you ate off his plate, again, when you know you can make your own."

“Paige, this the shit I’m talking about that Ezrah does.” I couldn’t do shit, but laugh.

We helped my mom set the table and called everyone in to eat. My mom had a huge house, and she made sure to have us over for Sunday dinner every week. She said grace at the table and told everyone to dig in.

“So, Paige, you seem to be happier this week. What’s that all about?” My dad asked, making everyone stop talking to listen.

“Yea, Paige, tell them why you’re happy, today.” Hope said, and I pinched her ass under the table.

“No reason, daddy. It’s just a nice day out, and I figured I can’t go around being mad at the world, because my marriage didn’t work.”

“I hear that.” My mom said.

“Well, I think her and Mark should get together. He’s only been after her for like forever.” My little sister, Janae, said.

Mark looked at me with this big ass grin on his face.

"Well, Mark had a chance, but he chose the streets. Plus, y'all know I been with Kamal forever."

"Ok, but you're not with him now." Janae said. I looked at Hope to help me out, and she stuffed more food in her mouth.

"How about we just eat and not try hooking her up with anyone." My brother, Eric, said. He and I were always close, and he didn't want me with anyone to tell the truth. He would rather me be alone than to be with anybody that would break my heart.

After dinner, my sister, Hope, and I helped my mom clean up. She gave Hope two plates to take home; one for her, and the other for her man.

"Paige, come back here in my room for a minute." My mom said, as I followed her.

"Yes, mom."

"I know you and Kamal are no longer together, but I also know that someone put that glow on you."

"Ma." I tried to speak, but she put her hand up.

"I'm no fool. I'm happy to see that you're happy, again, and I'm glad you waited until you closed that chapter in your life. Just be careful and don't throw your heart out there so fast for it to get broken, again. When you're ready to bring him around, or if you decide to, make sure it's on a Sunday. You know you're dad will want to talk to him, too."

"Thanks, Ma. I will, but right now, I'm just having fun. I love you, and I'll see you next week." She gave me the side eye.

"Ok. I'll try to come in the middle of the week."

Hope dropped me back off at home and promised not to say anything to Ezrah about what I had told her happened between Hakim and I. I made her ass promise, because I knew her ass pillow talks all the time with him. I ironed my clothes for work the next day and relaxed for the rest of the evening. I worked ten hours a day, as the General Manager at the bank. I was on salary and had to work at least fifty hours a week, so I made sure to get it done all week, so I could have the weekends off. I hadn't heard from Hakim all week, and I wasn't sweating it, because I didn't call him either.

It was Friday, and Kamal sent me a text, reminding me of our lunch date. I left work around 11:45 so that I would be there by twelve. The lunch hour traffic was just as bad as the damn late afternoon traffic. When I got to Red Lobster, it was a little after twelve, when I spotted Kamal in one of the booths. Thank goodness it wasn't too crowded, because I was hungry. We gave each other a hug and took a seat. The waitress came over and we gave her our drink and food order together. I already knew what I wanted, so there was no need to wait.

"What's up, Kamal? What did you want to talk about?" I asked, taking a sip of my Dr. Pepper.

"First, I just want to tell you how sorry I am that I failed as a husband and that I miss you so much."

"Kamal, you didn't fail as a husband. We were young, and neither one of us wanted to let go, so we stayed together for the wrong reasons. I miss you, too, because we used to be best friends."

"I wanted to tell you that I'm selling the house. I already found a place and have packed everything up. You will get half of what it sells for, and don't say you don't need it.

You're name is on the mortgage, so its only fair; plus, the judge said everything has to be divided up evenly."

"That's fine, Kamal. Do you need help packing? Hope and I can come help you."

"No. I pretty much finished it all. I do have a few boxes of stuff that belong to you. I can drop it off, or you can pick it up."

The lady brought our food over. We were eating when my phone went off. It was a text message, but I didn't know the number, so I had to open it up.

Unknown: Are you enjoying lunch with your man?"

The number wasn't saved in my phone, so I looked around the restaurant to see if I recognized anyone, but I didn't.

Me: Who is this?

Unknown: *This is that nigga that had you screaming my name and climbing the walls the other night.* I almost spit my drink on Kamal, as I looked around. I couldn't find him, anywhere.

Me: *Hakim?*

Unknown: *Damn, how many niggas had you doing that?*

Me: *No one; but this isn't the number you gave me at the club, because I have you saved in my phone. And, I haven't heard from you all week, so why do you care, anyway?*

Unknown: *It doesn't matter if I speak to you every day, or not. Just know I'm always watching.*

Me: *Yea, okay. Bye Hakim. I'll talk to you later.*

"Are you ok?" Kamal asked, now, looking worried.

"Yes, I'm fine. Let's finish eating so we can go. I'm going to use the ladies room. I'll be right back." I scooted out the booth and headed to the ladies room, which is when I ran smack into Hakim and some chick walking out hand-in-hand. The look on his face was priceless. I just shook my head, laughing. When I came out the bathroom, he was still standing there, but alone.

"Hey, Hakim. Where's your girlfriend?" He just scoffed up a laugh and whispered in my ear.

"That nigga can't please your body like I can. Isn't that the reason you gave it to me?" I shook my head, laughing, and crossed my arms over my chest.

"Listen, and listen well, Hakim." He stood against the wall with one leg up on the wall. I couldn't deny how sexy he was.

"Yes, you made me scream your name and even had me climbing walls, but don't get it twisted, boo. I can get the next nigga to do the same. What you fail to realize is that I'm ok with not fucking you again after last week. I'm not going to run behind you like these young ass girls do.

So, you can have that cocky attitude about your sex game all you want, but remember this; I know I had you weak in the knees with my head game. I also know I rode your dick like no other, because you were calling out my name. Yea, you thought I didn't hear you, but I did. Oh, and let's not forget, you made me breakfast the next day; so to say this pussy didn't have you feeling some kind of way seeing me with him, would be a lie."

I looked around the lobby area and noticed that no one was around. I stood face-to-face with him, put my finger inside my pussy, and gave him a taste. He sucked that shit like it was a lollipop. Thank goodness I had a maxi skirt on, so it was easy for me to go down through the front, instead of lifting my skirt up. Just as I did that, his little girlfriend walked in. yelling at him.

"It was good to see you, Hakim. Enjoy your day." I left him standing there stuck, and that's what his ass got for thinking that he could play me like I was one of those little ass girls.

"Kamal, are you ready to go?" I looked out the window and him and the chick pulled off. You could see that they were arguing, and I could've cared less. That nigga had the game fucked up if he thought he was going to play me. That is exactly why I didn't want to deal with someone young. The sex was the bomb, but he could miss me with the bullshit.

Hakim

I never imagined a woman that would have me hooked on her pussy after the first time fucking her. Paige had that bomb pussy. She may not have been experienced in some areas, but the ones that she was good at had a nigga open. I made her ass breakfast the next day, and I felt like a bitch after we had sex. Her pussy was so addicting that I had to have her again for breakfast and lunch.

When I turned my phone on, I saw all the messages. The first one was Ezrah looking for me. The next was from my soldiers on the block, and the last was from Noel's crazy ass.

Noel: *Hakim, when the fuck did you go out of town? You better not be laid up with a bitch. Call me when you get back.*

Noel: *Hakim, I miss you please call me.*

Noel: *Come over when you get back.*

The messages went on and on. That chick just did not get the fucking picture. I gave Paige a kiss, before I left and told her I would call her later. I had every intention to kick it with her during the week, but I couldn't get away from Noel's ass. She was everywhere I went, as if she was following me. I didn't want her to find anything out about Paige. Noel had fought every chick that she found out I was cheated on her with, and even though we were not together, I would never put Paige in that situation.

I was mad as hell when I saw Paige walk in with some cornball to have lunch. There wasn't really much I could say, because I had Noel with me. She wanted something to eat, and I was hungry, too, so I just brought her. I sent Paige a few text messages to let her know I was there, because it was luck that we were on the opposite side of the restaurant. Imagine my surprise that when we were leaving, she was going to the bathroom. I told Noel that I forgot something and gave her the keys to sit in the car.

When Paige came out the bathroom, I whispered some shit in her ear trying to piss her off, but the joke was on me, because when she responded, I stood there, stuck. Then, we she gave me a taste of her juices, I wanted to fuck her right there. Noel ended up coming back in, just as she walked away. Noel and I argued all the way to the car and when we got inside.

"I saw you talking to that old bitch in there. You think I'm stupid. What, you fucking her now?"

"Noel, I'm not doing this with you. It's over between us. I just brought you here, because I was hungry, too."

"Oh, it's over, but you weren't saying that shit last night when we were fucking."

"That was a mistake. You know damn well I was fucked up. Yea, I should've known better, but my little head thought for me. You got that, but trust me, that's the last time you will ever taste this dick, again."

"Yea, right. Can't nobody make you cum like me."

I just laughed, because little did she know that Paige's sex game was better then anybody that I had ever fucked with. I pulled up in front of her house, cut the car off, and tried to have a heart-to-heart with her.

"Noel, you have to let me go. This isn't healthy for you. You're never going to find another man if you're running behind me. I will always love you, but I'm not in love with you, anymore. I'm tired of you following me and fighting every chick that you see me talking to." She tried to kiss me, but I pulled back.

"Wow. You really want to end this?"

"Yes, Noel, I do. I need you to be okay with it."

"Listen, I'm going to give you time to think." She said, as she got out the truck.

Later, I was on the block, kicking it, when Ezrah called for me to stop by. He wanted to play the new Madden that had just come out, so I told him that I would be there in a few. I didn't make it over there until after ten, but that was fine. It was Friday, and he didn't have to work the next day.

"Yo', I'm outside." When I walked in, I was shocked to see Paige sitting at the island with Hope, drinking. That woman got more beautiful each time I saw her.

"Hey, ladies." I thought Paige was going to get smart, but she didn't.

"Hey, Hakim. How was your day?" I didn't know what to say.

"It was good. How was yours?" She put her drink down, walked over to me, and kissed my lips. She pulled my neck down and started sucking on my ear.

"I want you to follow me out this house and fuck me in your truck right now."

"You serious?"

When she nodded her head, I grabbed her hand and told Ezrah that I would be right back.

I let her hop in the back seat and locked the doors. She sat on my lap, unbuttoning my pants. I stuck my hand under her skirt, slid her panties off, and felt her wetness sliding down my fingers. I put them in my mouth and kissed her, then I lifted up so that she could get my jeans and boxers down. When she slid down, she was so wet that I couldn't hold out. Call me a minuteman all you want; her pussy had a man down. I took her breast in my mouth, one at a time, giving each one their own attention. She hopped off and went down, making my man disappear in her mouth. The more she sucked, the harder he got.

She climbed back on top and rode me backwards, causing her titties to flop up and down. I circled her clit with my finger and had her going crazy.

"Cum for me, Paige. Show me what I missed all week." That shit had her going buck wild. My truck was rocking like crazy, and the windows were fogged up, but we didn't care.

"Hakim, yes, yes, yes… Oh, shit. I needed that. Fuck me from the back. I want you to put all ten inches in there. She turned over, and I rammed my shit, hard in her pussy. She screamed out, but she took it like a champ. I smacked her little ass and watched it jiggle.

"Fuck, Paige, I'm about to cum." She turned around and put him in her mouth again.

"Mmmm, baby. Cum in my mouth." She started playing with my balls, going up and down, and before I could say anything else, I was shooting my load off down her throat.

"Open up, so I can have my dessert. I missed this." I said, licking my lips.

"Ugh, no. You won't be tasting her until I feel you deserve it. You have to earn that, boo." My mouth dropped open, when she opened up the door, stepped out, and stood there, waiting for me to get my clothes back on.

"Oh shit, Paige, are you really going to do me like that?" She waited for me to step out and gave me one of her kisses that made my dick hard.

"Don't worry. She is mad at me, too, for not letting you do it." She said, pointing to her pussy.

We walked in the house and saw Ezrah and Hope shaking there head.

"What?" I asked them, as Paige went to grab her stuff.

"Nothing. Y'all niggas couldn't wait until you got back to Paige's house?" Ezrah asked. I couldn't do anything, but laugh.

"Hold on, Paige. I'll walk you to your car." She said her goodbyes, and I walked to her car with her. She rolled her window down and let me kiss her.

"Can I come by tonight?"

"I doubt it. Your girl may not be too happy about that." She said, pointing to Noel, who was now walking straight to me. She pulled me in closer, kissed me aggressively, smiled, and left. That woman was doing something to me.

"What Noel?" I said, walking to my truck. She fucked my whole night up by showing up. I sent Ezrah a text and told him we would play tomorrow, because my stalker was outside, and I could see them look out the window. I pulled the blunt out of the console in my car and lit it up.

"So, you're going to fuck that bitch like we didn't just fuck yesterday?"

"Noel, I told you that that was a mistake, and what I do with my dick is my business. Why are you here? I told you a thousand times it was over."

"That's the same bitch from earlier, isn't it? Hakim, she is mad older than you. Why are you fucking her? She's like the same age as your mom."

"First of all, she's only a few years older than me. Second, my mom is almost fifty, and they're nowhere near the same age. If I wanted to fuck somebody that was sixty, that's my business. What does it matter how old she is, anyway?"

"Oh shit, you like her." Wait, until I tell your mom."

"Noel, go ahead with that shit. My mom doesn't care who I'm fucking. I'm out, yo'. You are becoming too psycho for me. Have a good night."

"Hakim, I'm going to let you have your fun with her, but I better not see her at your moms BBQ or any family functions." She yelled, as I got in.

I just turned the music up in my truck and left. Paige sent me a text saying that she was home. I wanted to go over there, so badly, but I knew that Noel was following me. I didn't want to go home, because she would bang on my door all night until I let her in, so I did the next best thing. I went to my mom's house. I called Paige and spoke to her for a few hours. Everything about her had me wanting to make her my girl, but I had to deal with that psycho bitch, first.

I knew that, the next day, her crazy ass would be over, so I was getting up early to talk to my mom. I always went to my mom when I had female problems, because she would always give it to me raw. Shit, she was the one that told me to leave Noel's crazy ass alone. I should've listened and now look. I turned on ESPN and tried to watch it but ended up dosing off.

Noel

Hakim thought he was slick; I knew that he was trying to get that lady's attention; that was why he sent me to the car. When I walked back in, I thought I saw him sucking on her fingers, but I doubt that he would do some shit like that in public. When I asked him about her, he pretended like he didn't know her. Now, there I was, sitting there, watching those two have a fuck fest in his truck. I must've been sitting out there for almost an hour, watching that truck shake. They lucky that it was a dead end street, otherwise, somebody would've been called the cops. I watched them walk in the house and come back out.

He walked her to her car and stuck his head in to kiss her. I was hot to death looking at him. I know that he said it was over, but I didn't believe him. He just got a taste of some new pussy, and he would be back just like he always did. She saw me coming towards them, so when she pulled him closer for a deeper kiss, I knew she was being funny; I had a trick for her ass, though.

Hakim and I argued for a bit before he left. I followed his ass just to see if he was going to her house. He ended up going to his mom's, because he knew I wouldn't dare bring any shit to her house, but as sure as the sunrises, I would be there first thing in the morning.

I woke up bright and early so that I could make sure to get there before he left, but that nigga was already gone. I knocked on the door, and when his mom came to the door, she had this evil look on her face.

"What's up, Noel? What's this shit I hear about you stalking my son? And, don't lie to me." I put my head down, in shame, because he got to her first.

"Ms. Jennings, I love Hakim, and I know he feels the same. I cheated on him once, and he can't forgive me like I forgave him all those times. I just don't understand why." I broke down, crying. I felt her rubbing my back.

"Listen, I'll talk to him. But, I can't make any promises."

"Thank you, thank you." I jumped up and gave her a hug. I was feeling real good, until I saw Hakim and that bitch ride by me, so of course, I followed them. They pulled up at Perkins and went inside. They weren't holding hands, or anything, so I could only assume that she wasn't his girl. I sat in the parking lot, watching them enjoy each other's company, when I couldn't take it anymore. I hopped out my car to approach them, when Hakim noticed me first and started shaking his head, which made her turn around.

"What do you want, Noel?" He said, as she looked me up and down, laughed, and excused herself to the bathroom.

"Yea, get the fuck out of here." She gave me this look, and I dared her to jump.

"Hakim, why are you here with her? Let's just go home. I miss us."

"Noel, this is getting ridiculous. You're about to make me disrespect you. I'm trying not to, but you're pushing me." I saw her coming back from the bathroom, then she took her seat.

"Noel, its time to go." He yelled at me, pissing me off, because she just sat there smiling and looking down on her phone. Just looking at her was pissing me off. I looked from her to Hakim and stood up.

"Don't do it, Noel." He said, which made her put her phone down and stare up at me.

"Hakim, I'm good on breakfast. Let's go finish fucking each other's brains out." She said. I saw the smirk on his face and lost it.

"I caught her with a two piece right to her jaw." Hakim jumped up, but it was too late. That bitch had me on the ground, pounding my head into the concrete and raining blows to my face. I was no match for that bitch. Hakim didn't even break the fight up; he just let her hit me. She got up off me and kissed Hakim on his lips, then she looked down at me and said,

"Honey, you're doing all this for nothing. Hakim and I are just fucking. Now, most chicks would look at me as competition and step there game up. But, you're being pathetic and begging for the dick. Yea, I know about Thursday, when he was drunk and you two fucked. The key word there was drunk. If you have to get a nigga drunk to fuck you, that's just sad. I suggest that if you want your man back, you bring your A game. I'm going to let you get that sneak attack, but just know that this old bitch fucking his brains out, making him leave your tired ass pussy alone. Oh, one other thing, If you ever put your hands on me, again, I'll put a fucking bullet in you. Now, have a good day."

I can't believe that bitch had just threatened me. That was ok, though. I had something for her ass. Her and Hakim wouldn't be messing around that much longer. I got up off the floor and waited for them to pull off. There was no way I was taking my ass back out there with her. I really fucking underestimated her, and she put an ass whooping on me.

Paige

Hope invited me over for some drinks after I told her about that bullshit Hakim tried to do at Red Lobster. Low and behold, that nigga stopped by, and since I was feeling a little tipsy and he had my pussy wet from the moment he walked in, I couldn't resist. We went out to his truck and fucked like rabbits. He was mad that I didn't let him taste me, but after that dumb shit he did, he had to earn that. I knew that he loved the way that my pussy tasted, so I knew it would have him feeling some kind of way.

After I left, he called me an hour later. He told me that she was following him, but he wanted to be with me. I told him fuck her, if he wanted to be with me, don't let her stop him, but I understood where he was coming from, because I didn't want to have to whoop nobody's ass. He showed up at eight o'clock that morning to take me to breakfast. We were enjoying ourselves when his ex came in, begging for him to take her back. I didn't know how he could have so much patience with her. I tried to stay out of it, because that was between them, but once she snuck me, all that shit went out the window.

"Paige, put this on your eye. I don't want you going to work Monday with a black eye." He handed me an ice pack from the freezer.

"Let me find out you box. You got some hands on you." He said.

"Hakim, listen. As long as you keep it real with me, I'll keep it one hundred with you. I'm not going to fight this girl every time I see her. I enjoy your company, and you know the sex is off the chain. If you want to keep fucking with her, I'm cool with that; just make sure that she keeps her distance from me. That's all." He looked at me like I was crazy.

"Paige, don't do that."

"Don't do what?"

"We been messing around for, what, a few weeks now? You know I'm feeling you, and I want you to be my girl, but I also know you just got out of a relationship, so I didn't want to force you into another one. Yea, you may be a few years older than me, but age aint nothing but a number. You should know by now that you got me strung out over that pussy. Why you trying to play me?"

"Oh, yea. Well, you can't force me into something I don't want to be in; that's first and foremost. But, you never asked me if I wanted to be your lady, because you assumed something that is far from what it is. I know I got you hooked on this right here." I said, pointing to my pussy. "But, trust me when I say, I'm hooked on what's in between your legs and what your mouth can do." He sat there, grinning. "Now, I think you earned your privileges back to taste her again." That man and me sexed each other for the rest of the day.

Ezrah and Hope came over to watch some movies with us, and when we told them what happened, Hope was mad as hell that she wasn't there.

"Girl, she better pray I never see her ass. She tried it." Ezrah just shook his head, because he knew how Hope got down for me.

"Well, Ez, I guess the chicks are going to be mad, now, when they see me and my girl show up at my mom's BBQ next week."

"Oh shit, who's your girl? I know y'all two niggas just fucking."

"Nah, this my lady right here. And, everybody is about to find out." I just blushed, as he told them.

"Hakim, what are you doing tomorrow?" Hope looked at me, because she already knew what I was about to ask.

"Nothing that I can't get out of. What's up?"

"My mom wants to meet you." Ezrah looked at him and shook his head.

"Her family is mad cool, but I'm sure her dad will want to kick it with you. Hope already told me her mom wanted me to stop by, so I'm going to."

"Yea, I'll go. What time?"

"Is 4:00 okay? That's what time I usually get over there."

"Yea, baby. Anytime to be around you is a good time." I just smiled.

We started drinking and were fucked up by midnight. Hope and Ez stayed in the extra bedroom, because we took their keys.

The next day, Hakim left early in the morning and told me he would be back to pick me up around a quarter to four, which was fine, because my mom only lived in the next town over. She was so excited when I told her that I was bringing someone to meet her. I sent my brother, Eric, a text so that he wouldn't be blindsided.

The entire ride over, I was nervous, and I didn't know why. We pulled up, and of course, everybody was outside. Hakim turned my face to his, kissed me, and told me to stop being nervous. Hope and Ez pulled up behind us, so I waited for her to get out. Hakim opened the door for me, just as my dad stepped outside. He shut the door, took my hand in his, and headed to the porch.

"Damn, that's your man Paige. He fine as hell. Does he have a brother?" My sister, Janae, said, as we got closer. I saw all her friends looking, too. Eric walked over to Hakim and gave him that man hug thing, while Mark stood there with his face turned up.

"Wait, you know my brother? Eric, you know him?" They just looked at one another and grinned.

"Mom and dad, this is Hakim. Hakim, this is my mom and dad." My mom gave him a hug, but my dad gave him a firm handshake and called him to the back.

"Already, daddy? Can't it wait until after we eat?" He gave me this look that told me to be quiet. I looked at Eric and told him to go with them. I didn't want my dad scaring him away. My dad had him out in the back for about an hour, but the good thing was that I heard them laughing, plus, Ez and my brother were out there, too.

"So, Hakim, you're the one that put the smile back on my daughter's face, huh?" I almost choked when my mom said that. I looked at him, grinning like a Cheshire cat.

"Guilty." I couldn't believe his ass was going along with that shit.

"Well, you make sure to keep that smile on her face. She's been though a lot, and seeing her this happy keeps a smile on my face, as well." My dad said.

"Well, Paige is one of a kind. I'm happy we found each other when we did. She makes me a better person, and she doesn't take any shit, I mean, mess from nobody. I hope she keeps me around."

"Aww, Hakim, that was so sweet." Hope said.

"If you keep making love to me like you do, I'm not going anywhere." I whispered in his ear, making him smile. When we finished eating, we got some plates to go.

"Baby, it's still early. You mind stopping by my mom's house? I want you two meet her."

"Of course, Hakim. Why would you ask me something like that?"

"Ez and Hope are coming, so you'll have her with you. She already met my mom, and they get along well." We pulled up to his house, and he opened the door for me and walked over to Hope, who had a blunt in her mouth. Hakim led me to the house with Hope and Ez right behind us.

His mom was in the kitchen, cooking and talking on the house phone. Shit, I didn't know people still had those. She had the one with the long cord to it and everything. I was going to make sure Hakim got her ass a cordless because that was just ridiculous. She hung the phone up, wiped her hands on her apron, and gave me a hug.

"Damn, Ma, I didn't even introduce you yet."

"You don't have to. This is going to be my grandkids mother and your wife. I just know it. Girl, you are gorgeous." She started laughing and went to hug Hope.

"So, you're Ms. Paige, huh?" I didn't even get to answer the first question before she asked me another one.

"The 'old bitch' as Noel would call you."

"Ma, are you serous right now?"

"Oh, boy, hush up. You know that crazy ass girl came over here and made it seem like she was a hundred years old when she described her. How much older are you?"

"Just a few years; I'm thirty-five."

"Oh, you and Hope are the same age. Oh, ok. Well, have a seat. Let me make you something to eat."

"Oh, I just ate at my mom's house, but I'll take a piece of that vanilla cake, if you don't mind."

“So, what are your plans with my son?” She asked, cutting the cake for me. Hakim sat against the counter shaking his head.

“Right now, we are taking it slow.”

“Oh, so y’all fucking each other’s brains out right now? There’s nothing to be ashamed of. All new couples do it.” I saw the faces my man was making, and I couldn’t help but laugh.

“Yes, we are, Ms. Jennings. We’re all grown, right?”

“That’s right, got dammit. Now, Hakim, stop acting like I’m embarrassing you and get with the program. I like her, so don’t fuck up.”

We stayed at his mom’s house for another hour, laughing; she was hysterical. She wanted all of us to come to her BBQ Block party that she threw once a year. She wanted to show me off to all her friends.

“Excuse my mom, Paige.”

“I actually like your mom. I’m probably going to be the same way with my son. I mean, that’s later on down the road.”

We rode to my house and that dumb bitch followed us, so he helped me out of the car, as she came over.

"Hey, Noel. How are you?" I think I threw her off by speaking. I'm not going to be petty about the shit. My man got the bomb ass dick, and I knew that she was going through withdrawal.

"This is the one and only time I'm going to allow you to speak with my man. I don't know why you can't take a hint, but that's your shit. Make no mistake that this right here is strike two. If you need to speak to him in the future, catch him on the street. With that being said, baby, I'll see you when you come in. Don't be too long, though. I need to feel him before I go to bed." I said, grabbing his dick. He turned me around and kissed my lips.

"Paige, I want you to stay out here. There's nothing she needs to say to me that you can't hear." Her face was priceless, but I wouldn't do that.

"I'm good. She came all the way over here to talk to you in private, but trust that, next time, there won't be any talking. I'll see you in a few minutes. Bye, Noel."

I didn't know, nor did I care what they were going to discuss. That woman was really going coo coo over Hakim. I understood that they were together for six years, but damn, when the nigga say it's over, just bounce. I was coming out the bathroom when Hakim came in with stress written all over his face.

"Let me guess. She's pregnant, and the baby is yours."

"How did you know? I didn't even get a chance to tell you."

"Hakim, why do you think she fucked you when you were drunk? That bitch had a motive from day one. What are you going to do?" He ran his hands down his face and laid back on the bed. I continued to put lotion on not letting it bother me.

"I don't know. I don't want a baby with her. She is stressing me out without one, and I can't imagine what it's going to be like when she has one. Are you mad?"

"Hakim, how can I be mad? Yes, we were fucking, but we weren't official. Do I think you fucked up? Yes. But, there's nothing you can do about it, now, but take care of the baby. Just know that if we're still together, shit aint going to be as cool as she thinks. We about to put some rules down with that. I've seen too many men go through this shit. The chick expects you to get her a house, a car, and all these other luxuries."

"Hell no! I'm not doing that! Her parents got money, and she has a car. I'm not upgrading shit for her; those days are over. And, what you mean if we still together? Remember my mom said that you're having her grandbabies and that you'll be my wife. Now, come over here and give daddy a ride before I hit these streets."

"You got that, baby." I took his jeans and boxers off and went for a ride.

The week flew by, and Hakim and I only saw each other when it was time to go to bed. He was out in the streets handling his business, and I was working my ass off.

Saturday morning, I woke up, feeling sick as hell. I thought it was my nerves, but Hakim wasn't trying to hear that shit. He ran his ass down to CVS and brought back all these different pregnancy test.

"I'm not peeing on those sticks, because I'm not pregnant."

"Paige, stop playing. I know you have to pee. If you don't pee on it, I'm going to stand right here when you go and hold it under there for you."

"Fine, give me this stupid ass thing." I snatched it, peed on it, and left it on the bathroom sink. Hakim peeked his head in the room with that dumb ass grin on his face, that told it all.

"Baby, I'm so happy you're having my baby." I had to smile, because I was happy too. I thought Kamal and I would have kids, but once things started going downhill, I stayed on birth control. Thank goodness I did, because we were no longer together.

"You know I got you pregnant on purpose, right?" He said, sitting on the edge of the bed, looking at the stick.

"What you mean, Hakim?" He turned to me with a grin on his face.

"The first day we slept together, we didn't use a condom, which was careless on both of our parts, but once I got a taste of you, I didn't want anyone else to have you. I made sure to release my seeds in you each time."

"You're right, we were careless, but even though you did it on purpose, it was my fault, too, for not making you wear one. I didn't want a baby, but I wont get rid of it, either. I'm glad you got me pregnant, though. I think we'll be great parents. When do you want to tell everybody?"

Shit, Ez and Hope already know. I told them as soon you said you weren't feeling well."

"No wonder Hope been ringing my phone off the hook. Hakim listen. This chick and me are going to be pregnant together. I'm telling you, now, I won't play second in your life to anyone except your mom and sister. I won't ask you to neglect that baby, but I am your woman first. Now, we can go to the doctor appointments with her, and we can get her what she needs for the baby. You won't be dealing with her by yourself from here on out. I'm not trying to tell you what to do, but if this is going to work, we need to have each other's back."

"Baby, I got you. You don't have to worry about me cheating on you or trying to be with her. You're all the woman I need. Now, get dressed, the BBQ starts in a few hours. We can tell your parents tomorrow at dinner. I'll pick you up around three, so be ready.

Hakim

I asked Paige to be my lady, and I was happy as hell that she said yes. Now, we were on our way to meet her parents. I helped her out the car, and when I saw her brother, Eric, I gave him a pound. Shit, I didn't know that was her brother. Him and his friend, Mark, were two of my most loyal soldiers. I was going to have to move him up a notch now that I was with his sister.

Her dad called me to the back, and I think Paige was more nervous that I was. Her brother walked back there with me, which she had probably asked him to do.

"Son, I'm not going to sugar coat shit. I know you're out in those streets, because you're name is known all around. I don't know how much my daughter really knows about you, but I would rather you keep her in the dark. She may be naïve when it comes to the streets, but she's not stupid, either. I'm not going to sit here and say that I approve of her dating you, but she is grown and she seems to care about you deeply. How long have you two been together?"

"We met the day her divorce went through. I think that was a few weeks ago."

"Yup, that's around the time she came over here glowing and happy. I know what you're doing out there, and all I'm asking is that you keep my daughter safe and guard her with your life. I don't want to see her hurt the way that other man did. I also know relationships aren't built to last forever, but if you decide to leave her, just make sure it's not because you were cheating."

"With all due respect, sir. I think I'm falling in love with your daughter. I haven't told her, yet, because I want to be sure that it's love and not lust. We both just got out of difficult relationships, and we are taking things slow. As far as protecting her, that's something you never have to worry about. Even if we broke up, I will always keep her safe. She doesn't know, but someone's always watching her. I know my name is big out in the streets, and I respect that you're not judging me. I'm trying my hardest to get out, but you know how the saying goes, "It's always easy to get into something, but it's a bitch trying to get out."

The night went well, even after we stopped by my mom's and she cut up. Paige and I were having sex that night, but something felt different. I didn't say anything until her ass woke up the next morning, talking about she didn't feel good. I knew her ass was pregnant, because her pussy felt different. I went and picked up a few tests, and I had to argue with her just to take it, but it was confirmed as soon as the pee hit the stick. I told her that I got her pregnant on purpose, and I thought that she would be mad, but she wasn't.

She just said that we were going to the doctor's appointments with Noel and that any more dealings with her required both of us to be there. I understood, though, because if she had a baby daddy before me I would feel the same way. I was on my way to pick her up for the BBQ when Noel called my phone asking if I would buy her something to eat. I'll be damned if Paige wasn't right about that shit.

"Hell no. You got a car; go get it yourself."

"But, I'm pregnant, and I'm tired."

"Well, I guess your ass aint hungry then. Not only that; what are you like a few weeks pregnant. Stop being extra already with that shit."

I blew the horn for Paige, and when she walked out, I didn't want to go anymore. She had on a fitted white mini dress; some strap up heels, and her hair was pulled up in a ponytail, hanging down her back. She was flawless, and nobody was fucking with her. She got in the car, kissed me on the lips, and told me to drive and stop staring.

"Hello, Hakim. I'm still on the phone."

"Oh, Hi, Noel. What did you need from my man this time?"

"Oh, baby she wanted me to bring her something to eat. She said she's pregnant and hungry."

"Ok, Noel, what do you want? We'll drop it off for you?"

"Nevermind, I'm not hungry now."

"Ok, talk to you later, then." Paige said, disconnecting the call.

"Paige, I don't know if I want you to go now. Damn, you bad as hell."

"Don't be like that, Hakim. I only have eyes for you. I'm doing the damn thing for an old bitch, don't you think?" She kissed me.

"First of all, you're not old, so stop saying that, and second, I don't want you leaving my side. I don't trust these thirsty ass niggas out here around you."

When we pulled up, there were cars and niggas everywhere. I parked the car, helped Paige out, and noticed all the bitches staring. My mom was sitting under one of the tents, talking to Hope, so we walked over to them. When they saw one another, they hugged and compared outfits. Hope was a bad bitch, too. There wasn't no mistaken about that, but my girl had her beat in my eyes.

I heard somebody call out my name, so I kissed Paige and walked away.

"What up, my nigga? That's you?" One of my boys asked.

"Yea, that's me. Pass the word for me. I want everyone to know that's me. If I even think a nigga staring at her, I'm putting him down."

"All right, nigga, damn. We get it. But, don't look right now, here come your psycho ass ex."

"Damn, I can't catch a break with her. Can you pull me away in two minutes? I know she don't want shit."

"I got you."

"What do you want now, Noel?" I'm sure it's something."

"Why are you treating me like this? I have been the best supportive girlfriend for you these last six years. And, now you act like I disgust you."

"You know what, Noel, let's go." I turned to my boy and told him to keep an eye out for that nigga, Mark. That was Paige's brother's friend, and since he heard about me and her being together, he been talking shit.

I led Noel to where my mom, Hope, and Paige were so that she could say what she needed to say. I was getting tired of that shit.

“What’s up, baby? Why did you bring her over here?” Paige asked. I knew that Hope didn’t know who she was, yet, because she would’ve said something to her.

“Noel, anything you need to tell me, you can tell my girl. All this calling me all hours of the night and sending me those nasty ass text messages is finished. Yes, she knows about all of them. We don’t keep any secrets.”

“Noel. Is this the bitch from Perkins?” Hope stood up, but Paige held her back. I had Paige sit on my lap, lit my blunt, and waited for her to speak.

“Noel, my son don’t want you. Why don’t you understand that? I thought you were a good woman for my son until he told me all the stuff you did to him, and then, to Paige. She didn’t deserve for you to hit her, especially, when she stayed out of it. Then, you went to her house for her man, and she gave you a pass for that. I don’t know how much longer she is going to keep her cool with you.”

“But, Ms. Jennings, I’m pregnant with Hakim’s baby… your grandbaby. Don’t you think he should step up?”

“Girl, you aint pregnant. I saw your ass out here two nights ago drunk as hell, falling all over the place with that whorish friend of yours. This woman right here is having my grandbaby, so if you don’t have anything else to say, get the hell out of here. I know you don’t want me to call your mother and tell her how you’re acting in these streets. Grown or not, you know she’s going to whip your ass.

I lifted Paige off my lap and told Noel to wait right there, while I ran to my truck. I handed her one of the test that I dropped in my truck when I brought it home for Paige.

“Let’s go. I want you to pee on this stick in my mom’s house.” She walked, slow as hell, inside the house. I was praying to God that she wasn’t having my baby. I waited for her to pee, and as we waited for the results, she started feeling all over me.

She grabbed my face and stuck her tongue in my mouth. Instead of me stopping her, I pushed her against the wall, kissing her back, forcefully. I lifted her shirt over her head, as she unbuckled my jeans. She pulled my dick out, and I sat back on the toilet and let her sit down on it. I sucked on her breast, as she went up and down just the way I liked it. I was about to cum when regret washed over me.

"Fuck, Noel! I can't be doing this. Get off me." But, it was too late, because Paige was standing there at the door. We were panting so hard that, I guess, we didn't hear her open it. She looked at me, then at Noel, then back to me, laughed and walked out. I didn't know what to think.

"Paige, stop!"

"Well, well, well. Now you see where that nigga's heart is really at." Noel yelled, standing behind me.

I pulled my clothes up and told her dumb ass to shut up and get dressed. I stepped outside, and it was dark out, but I still saw Mark grabbing Paige's arm trying to talk to her. I saw my boys coming from all different angles when they recognized him. They were by Hope's car, and I could hear him clear as day.

"Paige, what happened? Are you ok? What that nigga do to you?" I cocked my gun and placed it on the back of his head.

"Step the fuck away from her, before I blow your head off." My boys snatched his ass up so that I could deal with him later.

I could see the tears in Paige's face, and it tore me up. It didn't make it any better that Noel walked up and wrapped her arms around my waist. I guess Hope had had enough, because she went to jump out the car, but Paige stopped her.

"Start the car, Hope." She wiped the tears from her eyes and stepped out the car. She didn't scream or make a scene like I knew Noel would've if the tables were turned.

"Noel, this is what you wanted, right? You wanted Hakim? Well, guess what, you can have him. All the bullshit he put you through was a waste of time when he came back to you, anyway. I hope y'all have a nice life together." Paige said. I moved Noel's arm from me and walked up to her.

I took her hand so that she could walk by my truck with me. I tried to speak, but she wouldn't let me. I leaned back against it and let her talk.

"Hakim, I know you didn't love me, but you didn't have to do me like that. I told you that I would have your back no matter what, but the minute I turned mines, your dick was inside of her. It's okay, though, because I bet any of these niggas out here would love to play in this pussy." She said, now pissing me off.

"Paige, go head with that shit. I wish the fuck you would fuck with anybody out here."

"Oh, nigga, please. You can fuck who you want, and I'm supposed to be okay with that. Hear me when I say we're done. Don't bring your ass to my house, my job, matter of fact, don't even come to the hospital when I have the baby. I'll drop the baby off to your mom's house. You two can play house together again."

"Paige, cut the shit. You're not leaving me. This right here is forever. Just go home, and I'll be there in a few. I'm trying to be nice."

"Oh, so that's what you do? When you're being nice, you fuck your ex so she doesn't give you any problems. Without a condom, I might add, which is probably what she wanted, so that she could really get pregnant by you, but you're so blind or dumb that you fell for it. You two were made for each other."

"Paige, you better be there when I get there." I watched her get in the car.

"You know this entire time I've been standing out here; you have yet to apologize. Better yet, instead of making me get in the car with you, you'd rather stay out here with her, so if I didn't know where your loyalty lies, I know now. Pull off, Hope." She was gone, before I got to respond.

But, she was right, I never even said I was sorry, and I didn't leave with her. The one thing I could say about Paige was that she had class. Now that she was gone, I had to deal with Mark and Noel before I went to her.

Hope

I couldn't believe that that bitch, Noel, had the nerve to fight my friend in the restaurant. I didn't know why those young ass bitches thought that, because we're a little older than them, that we wouldn't beat their asses. What I did know was that that bitch better hope we didn't cross paths, because I was fucking her up on GP.

The day Hakim met Paige's family, I laughed the whole time. It seemed like everybody was okay with it, except Mark. I knew that it was because he was in love with Paige and had been since middle school. He tried to break up her and Kamal by saying he cheated when we knew that Kamal was scary as hell. Kamal was scared to look in the direction of another woman thinking that Paige would leave him. He worshipped the ground that she walked on, which is why when that shit happened that day with Noel and Hakim, he offered to let her stay with him in the extra room.

“Hope, can you take me home and help me pack up as much as I can. I told Kamal there was asbestos in my house, so he’s letting me stay with him.”

‘Paige, do you think that’s a good idea? You know that he is still in love with you.”

“I told him I was with someone else already. Plus, he’s letting me stay in the extra bedroom.”

“Ok, but you know you can stay at my house, because I’m always with Ez.”

“Good, I’m staying at your place then. I’ll cancel with Kamal. Does Hakim know where you live?”

“Hell, no! He thinks I moved in with Ez, since I’m always there.”

“Please don’t tell Ez where I’m at, and thank you. I love you, girl. I can’t go to my mom’s, because they’ll know, right away, that something’s not right. I’m going to call her in the morning, and tell her that I can’t make dinner, because I’m sick. Hurry up, Hope. I don’t want to be here when he comes, because I know I’m going to open the door.”

"Ok, come on. You have enough stuff for a while, and I'll come back in a few days to get you more stuff."

The minute we pulled into my driveway, Paige's phone was blowing up from Hakim calling her back-to-back. She called Verizon and had them change her number right away. She had to, just in case, he wanted to track it.

Before I knew it, my phone was blowing up from Ez. He was down the street, playing basketball, so Hakim had probably just told him what happened. I drove to his house, sat in my car, and texted him to say I was staying with Paige and would be home in the morning. I shut my phone off, before I pulled off, so they couldn't track my phone, either.

When I got back, my heart broke, as I listened to Paige in the bathroom crying her eyes out. I picked us up some McDonalds, and even though I knew she wouldn't eat, I still got her something.

"Hope, come here." She was sitting in the bathtub, with her knees up to her chest with red eyes. "Hope, why did he do me like that? I know I didn't deserve that." I put soap on the rag for her, told her to wash up, and we would talk when she got out. I didn't even know what had happened. She just told me to start the car. I couldn't hear everything that was said, because she didn't want everyone to know what had happened. After she got out, and was comfortable, she started telling me what happened. I was shocked that Hakim would even allow Noel to get that close to him.

"Paige, I don't know what I would do if I were you. I know it's going to hurt for a while, but whatever choice you make, you know I'm behind you one hundred percent."

"I know you are, and that's why I love you." I shut the light off to lie down, when I heard someone knocking on the downstairs door. When I peeked out the window, Hakim's truck was parked outside.

"Paige, get up, Hakim is here. What do you want to do?"

"I thought you said he didn't know where you lived."

"He don't. Ez must be with him. Listen, go in the extra bedroom. I keep that lock on it, because no one goes in there. I'm going to turn the TV up just in case." We moved all her stuff in my closet.

I walked down the steps, yawning like I had been sleep, when Hakim bust through the door taking two steps at a time. Ez just looked at me and shrugged his shoulders. I walked, slowly, back up the steps, dreading having to deal with his ass.

"Hope, where is she?"

"Hakim, she's not here. And, don't ask me where she is, because I'm not going to tell you. Just know that it's the last place you would think to look." He plopped down on the couch and ran his hands over his face.

"I fucked up bad. I never meant for that shit to happen."

"You damn right you fucked up." Paige said, walking out of the other room. Hakim looked at me, and I just shrugged my shoulders. She was putting her sneakers on when he got up off the couch to go talk to her.

"Stay right fucking there. I don't want you anywhere near me." Tears were coming down her eyes so fast that I don't think she was able to see straight.

"Paige, can I please talk to you in the other room?" Please." His ass was begging Paige, but she refused to give in.

"I'm not leaving until you talk to me." Paige looked at me. I knew what she was about to do. I walked to the door, and the minute Hakim put his head down Paige, hauled ass out the house. I shut the door behind her. Hakim kept asking me to move, and I wouldn't.

"Ez, get your girl, please." He asked.

Ez grabbed me away from the door, but I didn't care. I heard Paige when she pulled off. Hakim ran downstairs, but it was too late. He just came back up and sat back on the couch. I went in the kitchen to get something to drink and came back out to hear his side of the story. We sat there for two hours, waiting for Paige to come back. I turned my phone back on, hoping that she would call and tell me where she was, but she didn't.

It was after midnight when Eric called.

"Hey, what's up? What?! Which hospital? I'm on the way. Yea, he's right here. Alright, I'll be there." I started shaking and running around trying to find my keys.

"What happened, Hope? Was it about Paige?" Hakim kept asking me, but I couldn't get it out fast enough.

"She was in a car accident, and she's at the hospital." I couldn't finish my sentence before Hakim took off out of the house.

Noel

I was sitting in the drive-thru at McDonalds, when I saw Hakim driving by with that bitch, Paige, in his truck. I got my food and stayed a few cars behind them to see where they were going. He pulled up in front of this little ranch house; which I must admit, was nice as hell on the outside. The lawn was freshly cut; the flowers lined the front area where the porch was. I was assuming that that was her house if they came here. Watch me crush his whole world with the bullshit I was about to say.

"Hakim, can I talk to you?"

His ass was shocked to see me, but she caught me off guard when she spoke. I could give it to that chick; she would not come out of character; except for that day in Perkins. I knew that I could talk all the shit to her that I want to; I just knew not to put my hands on her, though. When he offered her to stay out there, I was mad, but I got over that, because she didn't.

"Hakim, I know you don't want to be with me, but I just thought I'd tell you I'm pregnant."

The look on his face was priceless. That was enough for me to walk away. *Now, let his ass go in there and tell his bitch that.* I thought. The next few days, I tried to get him to come over, but his ass wasn't beat. It was the BBQ Block party, and I didn't know how, but I was fucking him that night. When he asked me to take some test he had in the car, I was nervous as hell. My shit was about to blow up in my face if I didn't come up with a plan.

After I peed on the stick, I stared at Hakim; he had my pussy wet. He was, definitely, fine as hell. He had on some Dolce & Gabbana jeans, with a Polo shirt to match. He had on some brand new Tom Ford sneakers, diamonds everywhere, and some Tom Ford shades sitting on top of his head. I missed those days when he spoiled me with top designer shit.

I walked up on him, wrapped my arms around his neck, and put my lips to his. Shockingly, he returned the kiss, took my shirt off, and kissed me, as if he missed me. I pulled his man out of his jeans, slid down, and went for a ride.

"Hakim, this feels so good."

He guided my hips back and forth, but when he was about to cum, he started talking some shit about it not being right. He made me get up, but it didn't matter, because that bitch, Paige, was standing there. I didn't see her shed one tear. She just looked from me to him, and then laughed. Hakim went running after her, which made me mad, because I was the one fucking him. I snatched that pregnancy test up that I knew was negative, threw it in the garbage, and ran out behind him.

When I got out there, something had happened with Mark, because Hakim had the gun to the back of his head. I had to make note to find out what that was about, and why he was talking to Paige. Anyway, I put my arm around his waist when Paige stepped out the car to say she was leaving him. That bitch tried to put me on blast, though, when she said I was trying to get pregnant. I could admit that that bitch ain't no dummy.

Once Hakim told her that she wasn't leaving him, and that they were forever, I knew that the only way to get rid of her was if she died. I saw the hurt in his eyes after she pulled off. He went to his truck to smoke, and I followed behind him.

"Noel, why did you do that?"

"Oh, hell no, nigga. You're not about to blame this shit on me. You didn't have to kiss me back or fuck me, but you did. And, I know it's because you miss me."

"You know what, you got that. You're right. I did miss you, but not for the reasons you thought. I was so used to you following me that, when I didn't have to look over my shoulder, I wondered if you were okay. You're right, I didn't have to fuck you, and that's my bad. I don't know why I did it."

"I do. It's because you still love me. Why don't you just leave her and come back home? This is where you're meant to be. If you didn't want me, I would've never been able to fuck you." I saw him blowing smoke out his mouth, and I could tell he was in deep thought.

"Listen, we'll talk, again, but right now, I have to check on Paige."

"Are you serious, right now? What is it about her that has you running back and forth? Are you in love with her?"

"I'm not sure, but what I do know is that, I didn't have to do her like that. I'll call you later." I reached over to kiss him, but he turned his head. I knew then I had to get rid of Paige.

When he left, his mom called me over to her.

"What happened? Why did Paige leave like that? And, before you lie, I know it had something to do with you."

"Ms. Jennings, I'm not going to lie, but Hakim and I were caught in the bathroom having sex." I made sure to leave out the part that he made me get up. The look on her face showed me that she was disgusted, but I didn't care.

"Noel, I know you are still in love with my son, but what y'all did to that girl was dead wrong. I'm not blaming just you, because he was at fault, too, but that girl is pregnant, and you embarrassed the shit out of her. I don't know what's going on with, you but you have to get it together." She said, walking away, shaking her head.

Fuck that. Why was everybody worried about her, when I was the one that had been there for him? I jumped in my car and turned on Find my iPhone. I tracked that nigga to some house I had never seen before.

I stayed there for a few minutes when Paige came running out like she had been crying. I waited for her to get in the car and followed her. She was driving all erratic, so I pulled up behind her at the light, and put my high beams on. When the light turned green, I kept them on still driving behind her. She turned down some side street, trying to get away from me, but I kept going. I couldn't hit her car, because people would question why my shit was fucked up, so I would just run her off the road instead.

She was flying down the streets, trying to get away from me, and I loved it. It was only a matter of time, before she hit something, and I would be damned if her ass didn't run straight into the telephone pole. No one was out, because it was late, so I jumped out my car, and walked over to survey the damage. The car was smashed in the front, the windshield was busted, and the airbags had deployed. I opened the door, and there was blood everywhere. I checked for a pulse, but didn't feel anything.

"I whispered in her ear, "Hakim is mines. Now, die, bitch."

She couldn't hear me, but I felt it needed to be said. I shut the door, walked back to my car, and left. I was glad no one came out. I wanted her to die, and if someone saw it, the ambulance would come and try to save her. That bitch needed to die, and today was her day.

Hakim

I drove around in my car, for what seemed like, hours after that shit happened with Paige. I didn't know why I fucked Noel nor did I know why I didn't apologize or run after Paige. I had so much shit going on; then, to hear this nigga, Mark, was talking some grimy shit, because I was with Paige. To make matters worse, I went outside and that nigga was up in her face asking her questions about me. I put my gun straight to the back of his dome. If it weren't so many kids out there, I would've laid his ass out right there.

I had to go see what was up with that nigga. I parked in front of the abandoned house that we used to torture motherfuckers in, and Paige's brother was standing outside smoking.

"What up, E?"

"Not much. What's up? What happened with Mark? I got a call to meet here, and when I get here, they're dragging my boy in."

"Come inside. We're about to both find out what's up with his ass." When we got inside, there were a few boys playing cards at the table, some playing the XBOX one, and then, there was Mark who was tied up to a chair.

"Yo', untie his ass. There's no need for that." Mark looked up like he was shocked. I needed to know what his beef was with me since him and Eric had been riding with me for years; this was out-of-pocket for him.

"What up, Mark?" I said, taking a pull of a blunt that Eric passed me. He just nodded his head like he didn't want to speak.

"Mark, come outside. Let me talk to you for a minute. Yo', E, take this walk with us." I knew that that shit was over his sister, so I wanted him to hear it.

"Mark, what's going on with you? You been one of the most loyal niggas I know. I saw you at Paige's family house, and you gave me the side eye, all night. Then, I come out of my mom's house, and you all up in my girl's face asking questions about me. Never mind the grimy talk I heard you been saying behind my back. Care to explain?" I knew that

Eric had no idea by the way his mouth dropped when I asked him.

"Nothing man. Nah, fuck that. I've been in love with Paige since we were in middle school. She wouldn't deal with me, because I chose this life, only to fuck with the most notorious street nigga out there. Yea, I'm salty as hell about that. As far as talking grimy, I aint never been a nigga to talk about another. What you saw, was me asking Paige what happened; it was because she ran out the house crying, and since I know that's your mom's house, I knew it was because of you." He said, now passing the blunt back to Eric.

"Are you serious, man? You're willing to lose making all this money for my sister? Mark, you know, damn well, my sister gave you a chance back in the day, but you chose the streets; not to mention she wasn't trying to deal with your crazy ass baby momma. Yea, she may have picked a different nigga, but that's her choice. How you going to be mad at the next man for something he didn't make her do? Mark, you on some bullshit with that."

"You're right. I apologize, Hakim. We've been down for too long to go through some shit like this over a woman I aint never even had. You may not forgive me, and I know it probably just cost me my life, but I respect it. All I ask is that you keep my son safe."

Damn, I just looked at that nigga. I pointed my gun at his forehead, and then, lowered it. I couldn't kill that man, but I sure let his ass know.

"Mark, I'm going to let this slide, because you were in your feelings, plus you are a loyal nigga, and I can respect that; you knew what was up. But don't mistake my kindness for a weakness. The next time some shit like that happens, there won't be words. As far as Paige goes, unless you see harm being done to her, just know that it is none of your concern, or any other nigga's, unless it's her family."

We smoked the rest of the blunt, gave each other the man hug, and walked back inside like nothing had happened.

I called my cousin and asked him where Hope was. Once he told me that they were together, I picked him up to take me to her house. Hope wouldn't tell me where she was. I was talking to Hope when Paige walked in. Her face was red, her eyes were puffy, and the tears wouldn't stop falling, even if she had tried. I wanted to take her in my arms, but she didn't want to talk to me or even be around me. She ran out the house, but Hope blocked me from running after her.

"Why did you do it, Hakim?" I just ran my hand over my waves and looked down. I didn't even have a reason as to why I let that shit happen.

"I don't know, Hope. One minute, I was waiting for the pregnancy test to show the results, and the next I was fucking Noel. I didn't know Paige was standing there, so I don't even know how much she saw."

"She saw everything. She saw when she kissed you. The only reason she continued to stand there was to see if you would walk away. She didn't expect you to fuck her. She thought that what y'all shared was strong enough not to do it." I just shook my head and laid back on her couch. "You know what's bad, though, Hakim. She probably would've forgiven you, because she knew you were smoking and drinking a little. Not that it was an excuse to do it, because it was still fucked up, but you never apologized, and you stayed with Noel, instead of running after her to make things right."

"You're right. I fucked up real bad. I know I had a good woman, and I let Noel fuck that up." We sat there talking for a while when, Hope's phone rang. She was so hysterical that I couldn't make out what she said. When she was able to speak, I flew out the door after she told me that Paige was hurt. I did 90 trying to get to the hospital, and when I got there, her entire family was there, including my mom, and a few of my boys. I was a bit surprised that my boys were there, but if they were, it was for a reason. Her brother, Eric, walked up to me first.

"Yo', where you been? I been calling you for over an hour." I looked down at my phone and saw that it was dead.

"Shit, my phone died. I didn't know. What happened to her?"

"She hit a telephone pole. The doctor's haven't let anyone go back to see her, yet. We were on our way to the bar when we rode by and Jerome asked if that was my sister's car. We grabbed her out the car and drove her here; that's why it's so many of us. Hakim, she is pretty fucked up. There was blood everywhere, and I don't think she ran herself into a pole. Something doesn't sound right about that shit. My sister has never had an accident in her life."

I had to think about what he was saying. "Where the hell is Big John? He was supposed to be following her." I yelled in the ER making everybody look up.

"That's the thing. He was behind her, but said some car cut him off, running him off the road to get behind Paige. He said that there was no traffic, but somehow he lost her. I know you're upset, but Big John's taking this pretty hard, too. He knew that he was supposed to protect her and that he fucked up."

The doctor walked out and asked to speak to the Martin family.

"Hi, I'm her dad, and this is her mom. How is she?"

"Do you mind if I speak in front of everyone, or would you like to speak privately?" Her parents looked around and told him he could speak freely.

"Paige is going to be ok. She suffered a fractured arm, and some burns on the side of her face, from the air bag deploying, but that should go away. She has a huge lump on her forehead and a pretty bad concussion. Thank goodness she had her seatbelt on, otherwise, she would've went through the windshield, and we would be having a different conversation. We're going to keep her overnight for observation, but she will need to rest for at least a week." He said, shaking her parents' hand.

"Oh, yea, I almost forgot. The baby is doing fine. I guess the seatbelt protected both of them." At that moment, I felt like all eyes were on me. Her mom had the biggest grin on her face, but her dad wasn't too happy.

"Word, you and my sister about to have a baby? Congratulations." Then everybody else started in on the congrats.

I walked up to the nurses' station and asked if I could go back to see her, and she pointed in the direction of her room. I think that everybody was waiting for me to go first. When I walked into the room, she was turned on her side.

"Hey, Paige. Thank, God, you're ok." She turned over, and I could see the pain in her face, but I didn't know if it was from the accident or from what I did.

"What do you want, Hakim? Why are you here?"

"What the fuck you mean why am I here? When your brother called and said you were hurt, you should've known I would be here." She rolled her eyes and laughed.

"You came running after me, because I was in an accident, but you wouldn't come after me when you fucked that bitch. What kind of shit is that?" I knew that she was still dealing with the shit that I put her through. I scooted her over and got in the bed, and I was surprised when she let me.

"Let me ask you something."

"You can ask me anything." I told her.

"Do you still love her?" She caught me by surprise, because I wasn't expecting that.

"Paige, to be honest, I don't know. All I know is that that girl had been in my life for six years. When you asked me why I didn't chase behind you to apologize or check on you, it's not that I didn't want to; it's just that I was so used to her doing that to me, I figured you would do the same. When I saw that you weren't, I came for you, but you didn't want anything to do with me."

"So, you're telling me that you compared me to her?"

"No, I'm not saying that, at all, because she can never compare to you. I'm trying to tell you that what we share is different than her and I. I can't imagine what you're going through, but I would do anything to take it back. I should've been stronger and pushed her off, but I wasn't, and because of that, I hurt you. I do want to say I'm sorry, and even though, you won't forgive me, please know that I will always be here for you."

"Do you want to be with her?" I looked up at the ceiling, blew my breath out, and answered her.

"Again, I don't know. There's just a comfort zone when I'm around her. I mean, if I cheat on her, I know she'll come back, but you won't. No matter what I do, she'll still be down for a nigga, and I think I became comfortable with that. To be honest with you, I think that the reason I fucked her was so that I could keep her around, in case you and I didn't work out. But I regretted that shit, that's why I threw her ass off me. I know it sounds fucked up, but I wanted to make sure I had someone to fall back on."

"Ok, that's all I needed to know. There's going to be some changes in my life, as well, but I needed to see where your head was. I appreciate you being honest; I just wish you would've told me sooner than later. I gave you the chance to fall back from me, and instead, you moved forward already knowing you would still fuck around with her."

"I'm sorry, Paige."

"Ok, you don't have to say it anymore. When I needed you to say it, you didn't, so saying it now, because I almost died, doesn't make me feel any better. I thought we would've been great together, and I didn't want my baby to grow up in separate households, with step parents, but hey, as long as you have that stability with her that's all that matters."

"Paige, don't be like that. I'm going to take care of you and my baby."

"That's the thing, Hakim. You say that now, but how were you taking care of me and the baby when you were fucking her? Huh? You weren't thinking about us then. I don't give a fuck what nobody says; she was the one that ran me off the road."

"Paige, I know you're mad, but Noel aint that crazy."

"There you go taking up for her, again. Hakim, I know that, if I need something, I can call you, but don't wait on it. And, just know that I will not sit around waiting for you to make a damn choice between her or me. You let me know what it is, and I respect that. All I ask is that you respect whoever I choose to be with." I got up and looked at her like she had four heads.

"Paige, I'm going to say this as nice as I can. I better not hear about you messing with anyone, whether you're pregnant with my baby, or not. I told you, already, that this right here is forever." I said, pointing from me to her.

"Hakim, cut the shit, okay. This is over, and I'm free to do me, and you are as well. But, trust me when I say, if I find out that that bitch had anything to do with me and my baby almost dying, you can kiss her ass goodbye."

"Paige, stop that fucking with other people shit."

"No, you stop. This is over. You're not going to be fucking both of us until you decide what you want to do. I need you to understand that." I could see the tears running down her face like it was killing her to say it.

"Stop saying that, Paige. It's not up for discussion. This is not over."

"This is best for the both of us, so please, say that you understand, Hakim. Please. I'm not trying to hurt you, but I can't do this."

I was so mad that I punched a hole in the hospital wall. My hand was probably broken, because there was blood everywhere, and it was swelling up quick. Her brother came in, looked at me, then her, and shook his head. The nurses must've heard and ran in. I walked over to her, kissed her lips, and walked out.

When I left her room, Hope, her mom, and her dad, went running in. My mom came running behind me, crying when she saw all the blood on my hand.

"Hakim, you have to get your hand checked out. Honey, it has to be broken."

"Alright, I will, but I'm going to a different hospital. I can't stay here any longer." I dropped my mom off at home, after listening to her go off on me about Noel.

"Ma, I know Noel is not good for me. I don't know what I want to do right now. I need time to think."

"Ok, baby. I don't want to push, but you can't have both, so you have to pick one. Whichever choice you make, I'll support you. But, know that, when my grandbaby gets here, Paige and the baby will trump any chick you're with. Say what you want, but Paige is good for you. I love you, baby." She kissed my cheek and got out.

When it was all said and done, I had a broken hand. They gave me some Vicodin for the pain. I was in so much pain from my broken hand, dealing with two women, and that accident shit, that almost killed her and my baby I just drove to my house, took a shower, and passed out.

Paige

I heard Hakim when he came in Hope's house screaming my name, but when he sat his ass down, and said that he had fucked up, I had to make sure that he knew he did. I saw the surprise on his face, when I walked out, because Hope told him I wasn't there. After I ran out the house, I noticed a car following me. I figured it was Big John, because he'd been following me since I had been with Hakim.

I stopped at the light, when someone put their high beams on, blinding me. I tried to get away, but they stayed behind me. When I sped up, they did too, and when I turned the corner, they did too. I didn't know who it could have been, because I didn't have any enemies. I tried to lose the person, but when I turned down another side street, I lost control of the car and ran into a pole. I tried to get out, but the pain was unbearable. I thought I heard someone whisper in my ear, but I wasn't sure. I saw some lights, but I wasn't sure if I was dying, or not, until I heard someone talking.

"Yo', that's my sister! Help me get her out. We have to get her to a hospital!"

I could hear my brother, as I slipped in and out of darkness. I heard him telling somebody to call Hakim, while he called my mom. I wanted to scream out not to call him, but my voice didn't allow it. The next thing I knew, I woke up with Hakim standing right there.

He and I decided that us being together was not a good idea. Well, I decided, but he wasn't trying to hear that shit.

"Hakim, please say you understand. We can not be together."

"Paige, stop saying that shit. It's not over."

"Hakim, I can't do this."

I kept holding off on crying, but the tears were flowing without my permission. When he punched a hole in the wall, my brother came in, looked at both of us, and went to leave. Hakim came over to the bed, with tears in his eyes, kissed my lips, and left. That was three weeks ago, and I hadn't seen him since. My brother told me that he had been in the streets every day and stayed at his mom's house, just in case, shit kicks off.

That was one thing about Hakim; he didn't care how much money he had; he didn't have to be out there, but he liked being out there. He said that it eased his mind.

He wouldn't tell me if he had seen him with Noel, and it was probably best. Eric had been over every day to check on me, but I told him that, after that day, he didn't have to come anymore. I knew that Hakim was keeping tabs on me, but there was no need. Hope wanted to go out, and when Eric told me Hakim was going out of town, I agreed to go.

We pulled up to Club Mansions, in Brick, and the line was wrapped around the corner. Hope and I looked at each other like, 'we are not standing in that line. We got out and walked straight to the front of the line. The guy looked us over, pulled the rope up, and let us in. You could hear the hate as we made our way in. I mean, who wouldn't?" Hope was rocking a cream Alexander McQueen fitted jumpsuit with the boots to match. I had a black, mini Bodycon dress, with some high heel python sandals. We both had our hair out, and our makeup was flawless, so you see that they had every right to hate.

Of course, it was beyond packed, but Hope and I found a booth by the dance floor.

"Girl, it's mad niggas in here." She said, moving her body to the music in her seat.

"I know, but I don't think that I can deal with another young dude after that shit with Hakim."

The waitress came over, as we were talking and placed a bottle of Moet in front of us. She looked up and said, "Compliments from him. Hope and I looked up to the man smiling. He seemed to be an older guy, but I couldn't tell with all the people parading back and forth in front of him.

"Can I have a glass of red wine, and my friend here will enjoy this Ciroc." I asked the waiter.

"Girl, that better be all you're drinking, too. I know you're only two months, but keep it simple with the drinks."

"I know, Hope. Anyway, when are you and Ez going to have one?"

"Girl, bye. Ain't no kids coming out of here for him. That nigga still fucking that girl, Ashley, that works with him. He thinks I don't know, but I do. I went to his job one day after the gym was closed, and both their cars were still there, so I waited, and after about an hour, they came out hand-in-hand. He took her to her car and kissed her goodbye. To say I was hurt, would be an understatement."

"Really? That's fucked up. You're pretty much in the same boat as me. The sad part is that we are good women, and they don't know how to handle us. They can fuck around and do whatever they want, but let us do some shit like that, and all hell breaks loose. It's like they want us to wait until they're finished playing games."

I picked my drink up and made a toast. "From now on, it's all about us. Fuck those niggas." Just as I said that, the DJ made an announcement.

"Ok, everyone, let's give a shout out to Hakim and his crew that just walked in. And, I see he has a lady on his arm. Ugh, oh girls, it looks like the most eligible bachelor is off the market."

Hope and I looked at each other, then, to the front to see who the chick was, and wouldn't you know that it was

Noel. My stomach was in knots, when I saw him walking up to VIP with her.

"Let's dance." The song, "Supposed To Be," by Omarion, was on. We were killing it on the dance floor; we were grinding on the guys that sent over the drinks, when Hakim and I locked eyes with one another. I smirked at him and started getting real nasty with the nigga on the dance floor. Fuck that; two can play that game. I could see Noel trying to figure out who he was looking at, so when she saw me, I just waved.

"Bitch, you ain't shit." Hope said in my ear, still dancing with the other guy. When the song went off, we sat down. It just so happened that our booth was directly across from the VIP, butt on the ground floor. Hakim kept sending messages to my phone, and I kept deleting them. I wasn't up for his bullshit that night, especially, when he brought his girl. Of course, his sneaky ass sent Hope a message, and her dumb ass read it to me.

Hakim: *Tell Paige to stop playing with me before I come down there and snatch*

her ass up. I took the phone from her and lifted it up so he could see that I was responding.

Me: *Hakim, don't threaten me. You come in here flaunting Noel on your arm as*

your woman, but you checking for me. I haven't seen you in weeks, so stay in your lane up there. Don't worry. I won't let anyone fuck me, but they can eat my pussy."

I hit send and handed Hope back her phone. I laughed so hard that I almost peed on myself. When I looked up, Hakim was standing at our booth looking like a mad pit-bull.

"What the fuck you want, Hakim?" I said, picking up my drink.

"Paige, let me talk to you."

"Hell no! There's nothing left for us to say to each other. You made it clear where you wanted to be. Shit, you even upgraded her ass in some expensive shit trying to keep up with me. The only difference is I buy my own shit, and even on her best day, she could never be me. Hakim, go back to her, before you make me mad. I don't want my night to be ruined, because you over here on some dumb shit. Oops… looks like it's too late for that. Hey, Noel."

"Hakim, why are you over here in this bitch's face?"

"Yea, Hakim, why are you over here in this bitch's face?" Hope said, cracking up.

"I told you before, Noel, don't call her out of her name."

"You know what, Hakim, you and Noel can join us. Slide over, Hope." He sat in the booth first, and then her, and that's exactly what I wanted.

"So, what brings you to my table, Hakim?" I asked, grabbing his hand under the table and sliding it under my dress. Hope was texting on her phone, but was able to see, and shook her head. You couldn't see too much, because it was dark, but my girl knew what was up.

"Yea, Hakim why are you over here? You said y'all were done." She asked, not realizing that Hakim was now rubbing his fingers up and down my pussy. I put my head in my hands, as my clit started to swell. I pretended to be grinding to the music when, really, I was grinding on his fingers getting ready to cum.

"Answer her, Hakim." Hope said. He wasn't saying shit.

"Let's go, Hakim."

"Oh shittttt, Hakim, you better go." I yelled out when the orgasm took over. He got up to walk behind Noel putting his fingers in his mouth.

"Bitch, you crazy, as hell." Hope yelled over the music.

"Nah, a bitch needed that. Let me run to the bathroom to clean up. I'll be right back." I came out the ladies room, and he was on the floor dancing, with some chick while Noel sat up in VIP, mad as hell. I felt somebody grab my arm, and of course, it was him. We were dancing to "Drunk in Love," when he turned my back to him, so that he could wrap his arms around my waist. I lifted my head up at him, and he slid his tongue in my mouth, kissing me like no one was there but us.

"Paige, I miss you so much." I removed his arms from my waist.

"Don't do that, Hakim."

"What? I haven't been able to focus since you've been gone. I need you in my life."

"Nah, you got Noel."

"But, I don't want her. Do you think if I did I would be standing here with you?"

"The sad part is I don't know. You didn't want her before and look where that got us."

"What do you want me to do, Paige? Tell me; I'll do it." I walked away, leaving him standing there.

"Hope, let's go please." I glanced back and him, and Noel was in his face, yelling. He wasn't paying her any mind, as he watched me walk out the door.

Noel

The last few weeks had been pure bliss for me. Hakim and I were, pretty much, back together. Even though, he wouldn't put a title on it, I knew what we were. Since that bitch, Paige, was out of the picture, we could move on with our lives. Unfortunately, Hakim's mom wouldn't allow me in her house, so when he was over there, he would drop me off, which had been a lot, lately. Shit, he had even been staying the night over there, too, once I thought about it. Fuck it, though, he does live in another town, but all of his business was there, so he probably stayed to be close.

Since that shit with Paige, Hakim and I had sex a few more times, but he wouldn't fuck me without a condom or go down on me, anymore. Every time I asked him about that shit, he said, "You're not my girl. And, I don't know who you were fucking when we weren't together." I went to the doctor's office to make sure I had a clean bill of health, so that I could give him the papers, and we could get it in like before. Don't get me wrong, he's still fucking me good, but it's not the same. I'll chalk that up to him trying to get over me cheating.

Anyway, this night, we were going to one of his friend's parties out in Brick. He gave me some money to get a new outfit and to get my hair and nails done. He got the cast removed from his hand two days ago, and he was happy about that. He picked me up for the party around ten. We walked straight in to the VIP section. We were sitting in VIP, when I noticed him staring on the dance floor. I couldn't see who the chick was, at first, because her back was turned; she was freaking the hell out of some guy. I had to give it to her, the outfit she had on was bad, as hell. Imagine my surprise when I recognized that it was Paige.

What the fuck? I thought that bitch was dead. Why didn't I know she was still breathing? I was so deep in my own thoughts that I didn't realize that Hakim was standing at her booth. I marched right down there, demanding to know what the fuck he was doing. Every time I asked him why he was there, he wouldn't answer and just stared into space like he was deaf. It wasn't until Paige told him to go that he got up. He didn't follow me upstairs, because some chick grabbed him to dance. That was fine as long as it wasn't Paige.

Just my luck when I glanced back to him, Paige was in front of him, and his hands were around her waist. I had fumes coming out my ears when they stood there kissing, as if no one was there. She grabbed her stuff to leave just as I made my way to him.

"Hakim, what the fuck? You just going to disrespect me like that for her?"

"What are you talking about, Noel? You know that's my baby's mom, and there will always be a bond with us. Does she want to be with me? No? So, you can stop worrying yourself over it."

"Baby mom. Oh, she still pregnant?" As soon as that shit left my mouth, I regretted it. He snatched my arm and dragged me to the corner. He had me hemmed up against the wall.

"What the fuck you mean is she still pregnant?" Spit was flying out his mouth, as he spoke.

"Hakim, let me go. You're hurting me."

"No. Tell me what the fuck that means, before I snap your neck."

"I was just asking, because she was in a car accident."

"How do you know about the accident? The only people that knew was her family and a few of my boys?"

"Come on, Hakim. Just because they're your boys don't mean they don't talk."

"I'm telling you right now, Noel. If I find out you had anything to do with Paige and my baby almost dying, I'm going to kill you." He said, dropping me to the floor. "Now, get your ass up and go to the bathroom to clean yourself up. When you come out, you better act like you're enjoying yourself."

I couldn't believe that nigga was about to kill me over her. Fuck, I didn't know why I opened my big ass mouth. I had to cover my tracks the next time. And, trust me, there would be a next time; I was just going to make sure she was dead that time.

I washed my face, applied a little bit of lip-gloss, and headed back to VIP. This time, Hakim's whole demeanor changed, as if he didn't just have me hemmed up. The rest of the night went well, though. We stopped by his house, on the way back, to get him some more clothes. I went in the room behind him, wrapped my arms around him, and stuck my hand in his pants.

He sat down on the bed smoking a blunt, so I pulled his man out and slid my tongue up and down it. I could see him blowing smoke out, staring down at me. I spit on the tip, making it real wet, then he fucked my face like it was my pussy, and I took every inch in, like a pro, with no gagging. He shot his seeds down my throat, stood up, and pulled his clothes up.

I kissed on his neck and rubbed on his man to get hard, again. After a few minutes, he was standing at attention, again, so I pushed him back on the bed. He put his hands behind his head, as I grinded on his dick. I went to put him in my wet pussy when he stopped me.

"Hold on, Noel." I didn't know why he stopped me, until I saw him reach in the nightstand and grab a condom.

“Are you serious, Hakim? We’ve been together too long for this?”

“Do you want this dick, or not?” I was so horny I just jumped on it.

“Come on, ride that shit, Noel. I shouldn’t have to guide your hips.”

“Since when don’t you like to touch me when I ride you?” I said, still moaning.

“I want you to bounce on it.”

That nigga was bugging. He never asked me to do shit like that before.

“Fuck this. Turn over.” I did what he told me to do. He rammed that shit so hard in my pussy, I knew I was bleeding.

“Take this dick, Noel. This is what you wanted, right?”

“Yes, Hakim. Yes, just like that.”

“Throw it back, then. Make me cum.”

“I loved the way that he was talking. That dirty talk had me cumming back-to-back.

“Shit, Hakim, this is so good. Damn, baby, right there.”

"Fuck, I'm about to cum. He pulled out before he came. Ahhhhh...

"Hakim, why did you pull out if you had a condom on?" I asked him, as he was still trying to catch his breath.

"Don't start, Noel. Just enjoy the moment. Damn! You got what you wanted, and you're still not happy." He was right; I needed to calm down. There was no need in questioning him.

He ran to take a shower, before we left, and I noticed that he had more condoms in his nightstand. I poked a thousand holes in every last one of them. Fuck that; I was having his baby, too. We would just be pregnant together. He dropped me off at home and went back over to his mom's. I sat outside his mom's house until about five in the morning just to make sure he didn't leave to go see that bitch. I guess, she meant what she said when she said she didn't want to be with him.

Hakim

It had been three weeks since I saw Paige, and I was missing her like crazy. She didn't have a Facebook or Instagram page, so it wasn't like I could monitor her. I had been talking to her brother every day to see how she was doing. I was supposed to go out of town that week to meet up with this dude to set up shop in Philly, but I had a bad feeling about that shit, so I cancelled at the last minute, and I was glad that I did. I heard dude had some other cat from New York come down, and he got knocked as soon as he crossed state lines.

I had been dealing with Noel since Paige wouldn't see me. I knew that that was fucked up, because I should've fought for her, but I was still being selfish right now. Yea, I fucked with Noel, but I fucked this other chick a few times that I used to kick it with, too. I didn't want to take Paige through that, again, so I would just leave her alone for the moment.

I pulled up to Noel's house, and she came out wearing an all-black dress with a sleeve on one side. I wasn't sure as to what the brand was, but she looked nice. She could never match Paige's fly, though, no matter how hard she tried. Paige could walk out in some sweats and a wife beater and still be flawless.

I walked in the club and, instantly, got mad when the DJ announced that I had a girl. I didn't even hold her hand when we got there; she could've been with anyone. It didn't matter, though, because chicks liked fucking with a man if they had a girl. I stepped in the VIP section, when I spotted Paige on the dance floor freaking the hell out of some guy. When we locked eyes, it was like she was the only one there. I went to her table, after the text she sent from Hope's phone. She was being smart when she invited Noel and I to sit. I didn't care, though, I was able to make her cum. I pulled her on the dance floor, and she left me standing there. I swear that woman had me stuck on stupid when I was around her.

I stopped by my house to get some clothes when Noel decided she wanted to fuck. I let her suck my dick, and I fucked her just like she was a chick off the street. Sex with her didn't even feel the same. I thought about Paige each time we did it. She had the nerve to get mad, because we used condoms.

She lost her damn mind if she thought, for one second, that she was having my baby. That spot was reserved for one woman, and at that moment, she wasn't fucking with a nigga.

The next day I needed to run home for something, so I brought Jerome with me. I checked my surveillance tapes when I saw Noel do some foul shit. I was so mad I had to show my boy.

"Yo', man, that girl is tripping. You need to get rid of her ass. It's clear she trying to trap your ass."

"I know. I'm just comfortable with her, because I know she'll be down for a nigga."

"What happened with you and Paige?" I told him the entire story, and he just shook his head.

"So, you did all that because you thought Paige would leave you? Bro, she stuck around you after the fight in Perkins, all the times Noel showed up, and when Noel said she was pregnant. You picked this grimy bitch over her? I don't know what type of loyalty you feel you owe Noel, but Paige sounds more like a ride or die to me. It's clear as day that Noel doesn't want you to be with any other chick, so she's sabotaging your life."

"Yo', that shit funny as hell that you say that. When Paige got into that accident, she laid in the hospital bed and told me that she thought Noel did it. I told her she was bugging, but then, last night, Noel asked me was Paige still pregnant, because she was in an accident."

"How did Noel know about the accident? It was only a few of us there, besides family, and you know aint none of us talk. When we found Paige, that shit didn't look right, so we made sure we kept that quiet, so we could find out if someone tried to kill her." I ran my hands over my face, blew my breath, and laid back on the couch. I didn't want to believe that Noel would do something like that, but you never know.

"Keep this shit under wraps, until we know for sure. I think Paige will really kill her, if she found out. Not that I would blame or stop her, but I want to be sure." He nodded is head, and we left. It was a little after ten, and I told Jerome to drop me off at Paige's house. I knew that Noel's ass thought I was with him, so she wouldn't be following me around. I was nervous, as hell, walking to the doorstep. I rang the doorbell a few times before she answered.

"What Hakim? Do you know what damn time it is?" She yelled through the screen door.

"Open the door, Paige, I just want to talk to you." She unlocked the screen so that I could come in. She stepped aside and allowed me to pass. I sat on the couch while she locked up, then she went to her bedroom and got back on the phone.

"Hope, I'll call you back." She said, putting the phone on her nightstand and getting under her covers.

"You weren't even sleep." I said, sitting on the bed and lying back.

"Hakim, what is it? You seem stressed out. Let me guess, your boo did some foul shit, and now, you think you're running back over here."

"You can't even imagine the foul shit she did. And, I'm not running back to you, because you don't want me. I just miss talking to you." She rubbed her hand over my head and kissed my forehead.

"What happened?" I started telling her the shit I had been going through, leaving out the part about the accident. I told her about Noel putting holes in the condom, and she laughed so hard she started coughing.

"That shit ain't funny, Paige."

"Well, that's what happens when you pick a chicken head to be your main chick." I had to grin, because she was right. I was so busy being selfish that I didn't realize that what I needed was right in front of me.

"Have you felt the baby kick, yet?" I asked, rubbing her stomach.

"I'm not sure. I feel these flutters all the time, but I don't know if that's a kick. It does feel weird having another person in my stomach. Do you want to see a picture of the baby?" She was so excited about being pregnant.

"Girl? I can't tell what this is."

"I know, me either. I just know it's a baby." She said and busted out laughing.

"Paige, do you think you could ever forgive me and find your way back to me?" The demeanor in her face changed as soon as the question left my mouth.

"To be honest, I've been missing you like crazy. And, seeing you last night in the club brought all my feelings back to surface. I know you didn't mean to hurt me; shit, I know you didn't expect me to see y'all fucking, either."

"I don't know if I could ever trust you. I never questioned you when you were out, but if I were to be with you, again, I would worry if you were with another woman. You know me; I'm not the type to chase a man, and I'm not about to start."

"I understand. I need you to understand that no other nigga better be in here."

"Nigga, you don't pay any bills up in here."

"You heard what I said." I started tickling her, and she almost fell out the bed trying to get away.

I stood up and pulled her to me. "Is it ok if I stay over?"

"Yea, but your ass staying in the other room. At least, I'll know you're safe and not giving this away." She said, grabbing my dick.

"This is all yours when you want it." She stood on her tip-toes and placed a kiss on my lips.

"I still have some of your clothes here. I think you have some basketball shorts here, too. Look at the top of my closet."

"Aww, and you cleaned them. Thanks, baby."

She gave me a towel and went back into her room. I let that hot water hit my body full blast. By the time I got out, Paige had her light out, but the TV was still on. I went into the other room, turned on the television, and thought about how my life was so fucked up, because of Noel and my being selfish.

Paige

I was on the phone with Hope when somebody started ringing my doorbell. I looked at the clock, and it was 10:15. I let the person stand out there, because I wasn't expecting anyone. The person continued to ring the door, and I knew who it was. I didn't even look out the peephole. When I opened the door, Hakim stood at the door looking damn good. That man was, definitely, my weakness, for sure.

I let him come in, because if I would have left him standing out there, he would have probably broken the door down. We sat up for a while, talking, laughing, and joking. I showed him the baby's ultrasound picture and neither one of us had an idea of what the hell we were looking at. He tickled me so badly that I almost fell off the bed. I handed him a towel, and his clothes to shower, and went to bed. Well, I laid there, watching television.

I saw him look into my room, and he had on some basketball shorts and a towel wrapped around his neck. His body was calling me, but I refused to go to it. I tried to sleep, but it wouldn't come to me. When I looked at the clock, it was 12:30. I tip-toed to the kitchen to get some water, and then, I peeked into his room, where he was still watching TV. I smiled at him and went back into my room, putting my water on the nightstand. When I turned around, he was right behind me.

He lifted my chin, parted my lips with his tongue, and gently, sat me on the bed.

"Hakim, I don't think this is a good idea."

He ignored me, got on his knees, and scooted my body closer to his face. We started to kiss each other, hungrily, then he stuck two fingers inside, causing a moan to escape my lips. I leaned back, but he pulled me back up.

"I want you to watch me, baby." He said, as he started sucking on my clit. His fingers found my g spot provoking my orgasm to come sooner than later. I erupted like a waterfall down his face, then I watched him lick my juices and dove back in.

"Damn, you taste so good. Mmmm, I missed this pussy, girl. Cum in my mouth."

"Oh, Hakimmmmm. It feels so good. Don't stop. Here I cummmmm."

He stood, lifted me up, and guided me down on his long pole. He sucked on my neck and moved down to my breast, as I went up and down.

"Aaaahhh, fuck, Paige. Your pussy is the only one that feels right when I'm inside. Ride it, baby. Just like that…" He said, watching me take control. He loved that he didn't have to guide my hips.

"Hakim, I want to cum with you. Make me cum with you."

He massaged my pearl with his forefinger. I exploded on him, and in return, he did the same inside me. Once we were finished catching our breath, I took his man in my mouth. I sucked on his rod and massaged his balls in my hand. I ran my tongue inside the tip, bringing him closer to his orgasm. He observed me make his man disappear and went crazy.

"Mmm, Hakim, your dick taste so good. I want you to let it go. Cum for me, daddy." This nigga had his hands over his face, and his leg was shaking.

"Oh, my God, Paige. I can't take anymore." I made the sucking and slurping noises that he liked, too.

"I'm cumming, Paige. Suck that shit. Aaaaaah, yea…." I saw his eyes roll, as he shot his hot liquid down my throat, and I sucked every last drop.

I swear, he was ready to curl up in a fetal position from how hard he came. I laid next to him, and he didn't want me to touch him, yet, as his body was still calming down from that powerful orgasm. I knew that he was down for the count, so I showered and brushed my teeth. He was knocked out when I got out the shower, so I turned the TV off and snuggled underneath him. He wrapped his arm around me and kept it there all night. Lord knows I missed him.

The next day, Hope got to my house around 8:30, and Hakim was still asleep. I had the front door opened, so that she wouldn't wake him ringing the doorbell. I knew he needed the rest, so I closed the door, and left him alone.

"Hey, are you ready? I don't want to be in the nail salon all day."

"Hope, we have 9:00 appointments, so we won't be there long. You don't have shit to do, anyway, so what are you complaining about?"

"Anyway, bitch. What did Hakim want last night? I see his truck ain't here, which means he didn't stay the night."

No, bitch, he's here. I put that ass to sleep last night, and he hasn't woke up yet." I told her, slapping her hand.

"Ok, now. Does that mean y'all are back together?"

"I don't want to jump back into anything right now. I'm ok with just being his friend and an occasional fuck buddy."

"Ok, but once Noel finds out, you're going to be in the same shit. Just be careful, and know, I have your back."

"I know you do. Let's go."

"Yea, let's go with them damn hickeys on your neck."

"I know, girl, and I told his mom I would stop by today. You know she's going to have some shit to say." I left Hakim sleeping and sent him a text message.

Me: *Hey, you. I had a wonderful time last night. You see I put that ass to sleep. If you need me, just call. Have a good day.* ☺

We left the nail shop after eleven and decided to grab something to eat from Joe's Crab Shack since we were right by it. We didn't stay there long, because I felt like the food wasn't cooked well. Hope parked in front of Hakim's mom's house, and we saw him just getting out of his boy Jerome's car. He didn't even close the door before Noel was running up to him.

"What Noel?" He didn't take his eyes off me, as she stood in front of him talking. I started blowing kisses in his direction.

"Hakim, where are you going?"

"Bitch, stop fucking with him like that." She grabbed my arm and strolled into his mom's house.

"Don't think I don't see those hickeys on your neck. Are they from my son?"

"Of course they are. I would never sleep with another man right now."

"I wish y'all hurry up and make up. He over here every night stressed out over you. That girl driving him crazy."

"I know. When it's time for us to rekindle what we had, we will. Until then, I'm hungry." She made us spaghetti with salad and garlic bread for dinner. Hakim came in and sat next to me rubbing my stomach.

"Wait, where's your girl?" I said, placing my leg on his under the table.

"My girl sitting right here, carrying my baby. She just taking her time to find her way back to me, that's all." I leaned over and kissed him.

"Soon, baby, soon." I said, making him smile.

"That bitch can't come in my house anymore. What she did at the BBQ was disrespectful, not only to you, but to my damn house. She can't step foot in here."

"Wow, baby. You sure know how to pick them."

"I picked you, though."

"No, I picked you. When you're ready to be with me and only me, I may be there. But, if you take too long, that's going to be on you. I do miss you, though, so don't take too long." I said, kissing him again.

"Get a room." Hope said.

Ezrah walked in, and Hope's facial expression changed. He kissed her on the cheek, and her body cringed from his touch.

"Ok, Hope, can you take me home?" I knew she didn't want to be around him, so I made up an excuse for us to go."

"I'll talk to you later. Thanks for the dinner, and I'll try and stop by once a week before I get too big."

"Ok, sweety. I'm rooting for you and my son."

"See you later, Ez." He gave me a hug and kiss on the cheek. Hope went out to the car before me, so when I asked if she was ok, she broke down, crying. It was getting dark out, so I volunteered to drive.

Hope

"Paige, hurry up. I want all my stuff out of here before Ezrah gets off work. Matter of fact, let's finish and head over to his job. I am finally going to confront him about that shit, and I hope she's there with him."

"Hope, you know I got your back, but are you sure this is what you want to do? I'm just saying, you said you know for sure that he's still fucking her, but are you ready for him to confirm it?"

"Paige, I don't need confirmation. I just want him to know I know; that's all. You know I can accuse him all I want, and he'll just deny it, but if I catch him in the act, there's nothing to deny?"

"Ok. Just remember what I went through when I caught Hakim fucking that chick. That shit had me heartbroken for days."

"I know, Paige, but you got passed it. I don't know if I can, because he's been lying the entire time. At least, Hakim was with you every day and not giving you any reason to question him until that day."

"Yea, I guess you're right. Look… His ass texting me right now." She showed me the text of him, begging for her to take him back. I had to give it to her, though; she remained classy throughout the entire thing.

After we packed everything up, we dropped it off at her house. I ended up moving out of my apartment when she got in the accident, because I wanted to be close to him, but that shit backfired, quickly. Paige and I were going to be roommates.

It was now 11:00, and Ezrah's and Ashley's car were still in the parking lot, and it was closed. Paige and I walked to see if the front door was locked, and luckily, it wasn't. Those idiots must've forgotten to lock the door. We walked in and headed to the back where his office was. The door was cracked, so Paige and I peeked in. Ezrah was sitting in his chair, smacking Ashley on the ass, as she rode him. They were butt ass naked, as if they were at home. Paige gasped, so I pulled her back, because I didn't want them to know we were there, yet.

I had Paige sit in a chair with me outside his office until they were finished. You could hear skin smacking and moaning. I sat there, crying my eyes out, and she tried to get me to leave, but I needed him to see my face. It may sound crazy for me to not say anything, but listening to how much he enjoyed it, made it easier for me to hate him. And, that hate would ensure that I would never take him back. At least, Hakim had the strength, at some point, to push Noel off. That nigga had her cumming back-to-back, as did she, like he didn't have a chick at home. When they finally finished, I wiped my eyes with the back of my hand and stood up.

I sent his ass a text message.

Me: *Hey babe, you coming home soon. I miss you.* I had my phone on silent, so I could see if he would respond.

Ezrah: *Yea, baby. I'm on my way. I miss you, too. Be ready to give daddy what he*

wants. I couldn't believe this motherfucker thought he was going to fuck me after he just fucked her. That shit had me thinking about how many times he did that. I was sick to my stomach. I heard him talking to her when what she said next knock the air out of me.

"Baby, when are you going to leave her? I don't want to keep sleeping without you. And, you said you'll be with me when the baby comes."

"I know, Ashley. Just give me some time." I had had enough. Just as I was getting ready to go in, she opened the door and smirked when she saw me standing there. Ez just stood there with his mouth hanging open.

"Hope, how long have you been out there?"

"Long enough. I didn't want to interrupt your fuck session, so I waited, but it looked like I found out more than I wanted to. Ashley, how many months are you?" she grinned and said four months. I looked down at her stomach and saw she was poking out a little.

"Let me explain, Hope. It's not what it looks like." Ashley stood there, with her arms crossed, waiting for him to answer. Paige was standing right there making sure she didn't try anything stupid.

"Ashley, you can go. I need to talk to my lady."

"Oh, now, she your lady? That's not what you were saying when we were fucking, but okay. Call me when you're done."

"Bitch, get the fuck out." Paige said, pushing her out the door.

"I know you don't think I'm leaving. Whatever you have to say to Hope, you may as well say it."

"Ez, there's no need for any words to be spoken at this point. I've known for a while that you two been fucking. I had to find the strength to confront and leave you. Tonight has been more than an eye-opener for me. I took a chance on loving you, because you promised never to hurt me. What was it that you said, 'Age aint nothing but a number? And a real man doesn't have to cheat on his woman when she gives him the world and mind-blowing sex.' That's what you said, right, and you told me I was that woman. But, I guess all that flew out the window when you started fucking Ashley, again. Ez, I hope y'all have a good life together, and congratulations on the baby." I wanted to hit him so badly, but what would that solve?

"Hope, come back. You're not leaving me. We can work this out?" He grabbed on my arm, and I yanked it away.

"Are you fucking serious? You just told that girl you were leaving me. I did you a favor and moved out already. Don't call me or text me shit! Forget you even know me."

"Hope, please. I don't want to live without you." This nigga pinned me up against the wall kissing my neck. I tried to fight him, but he just grabbed my hands and put them over my head. Paige was punching him, but I told her to stop. I didn't want anything to happen to the baby. Hakim walked through the door a few minutes later pushing him off of me. I figured Paige called him, because she wasn't able to help me.

"What the fuck is going on, Ez? Why you got her hemmed up like that?" When he wouldn't answer, Paige told him.

"Damn, Hope, I'm sorry. Yo', Ez, didn't you learn anything from what I went through with Paige?" Go ahead Paige and take Hope with you. I'll call you later."

"Hope, I'm telling you this ain't over. I better not see you in another nigga face, either."

I didn't want anything else to do with him. Paige dropped me off at the bar and went home. I ordered me a cranberry and vodka drink and went to play pool. I bent over to shoot the ball, when I heard a familiar voice talking to me.

"Somebody must've really pissed you off if you're out here drinking and playing pool alone." I knew that voice so well.

"Hey, you. What's up?" I asked, giving him a hug.

When we pulled back from one another, I noticed how sexy he was. He stood there looking like a young Blair Underwood in his crisp black t-shirt, denim Armani jeans, and the new Prada laceless sneakers. He had a gold chain around his neck, his hair was freshly cut, with waves that would make you seasick; And, he smelled so good.

"What you doing out here, and where's my sister?" Eric asked, licking his lips, as he sized me up.

"I dropped her off at home. I wanted to be alone so I came here."

"What that nigga do now? I swear y'all be picking the wrong motherfuckers. Don't get me wrong, I know what

Hakim did to Paige, but she's grown. As long as he don't put his hands on her, I don't get involved. But, what's up with you? You still with that nigga?"

"Nah, that shit is over. I think his betrayal goes deeper than what Hakim did." I said, sipping on my drink. We stayed in the bar until closing time. I was a little fucked up, so he had to take me home; but I didn't want to go inside. Hakim's truck was there, and I knew that they would be fucking.

"Eric, can I come over just for the night? I don't want to go in. They are trying to work shit out, and I'm not beat to hear them."

He just laughed and took me to his house. He stayed in a condo by the beach, and to say it was anything less than nice, would have been an understatement. The condo was on the sixth floor and had a huge kitchen and living room; there were two bedrooms, two bathrooms, and a balcony, with a beach view. He had it laid out with a gold and black décor throughout the house. There were family pictures all over, as I gave myself a tour. I walked up to the fireplace and picked up one in particular.

"Eric, what are you doing with this picture?" It was a photo of him and me in high school. We used to flirt with each other, but never pursued it, because he was in the streets, and I left for school. When he didn't answer, I went to see what he was doing, and he was stepping out the shower. I tried to turn around and walk out, because the way his body was cut-up, and seeing the water dripping on his chest, had me wanting to jump on him.

"What's up, Hope?" He asked drying his chest off with a separate towel. I didn't realize how much I was staring until he smacked my leg with the towel.

"Uhh, I was just asking where did you get this photo from?" He opened up his drawer to take some clothes out. I just sat down on the edge of the bed, waiting for an answer.

"Oh, I kept that picture, because we used to have so much fun back then. It was always you, my sister, Mark and I. We were thick as thieves, until you two left for school, and then, we dove, head first, into the drug game. It reminds me of how innocent we used to be every time I look at it. Why?"

"No reason. I was just shocked to see it. That's all."

"Ok, can I get dressed, now, or are you going to sit there and watch me?" He asked, laughing. I just asked him for a towel and left.

Eric

Ok, I know you guys are wondering why I had a picture of Hope in my house. Hope was my first love, and before you say anything, she didn't know it. She was my sister's best friend and three years older than me. I had a crush on her since I was younger, and when she left for school, I tried to tell her, but I knew she wouldn't look at me like that, so I kept my feelings hidden. I was about to be a sophomore, and she would be freshman in college. I knew she wasn't going for that. We would hang out on the porch all night with them until my mom made us come in.

When her and Paige would come home, I made sure I stayed around the house as much as possible. When I turned 21, we went out to celebrate and kept in touch, but then years passed, and I would only see her on Sundays when my mom would cook a big family dinner. After a while, I pushed her to the back of my mind, because when she was single, I wasn't and vice versa.

Over the last year, she had been with that nigga, Ezrah, who I knew was Hakim's cousin. I knew he was cheating, because it had been plenty of times that Hakim and I went to his gym, and he would be in his office fucking some chick that worked there. It wasn't my business, and what did I look like snitching on a nigga.

Now, here she was at my house, because that nigga had fucked up. I had just broke up with Brittany a month ago; she wanted a nigga to marry her, and I just wasn't that dude. I had only been with her for six months, and she wanted to lock my ass down. When I saw Hope in the bar, I secretly prayed that that nigga had fucked up, and to my surprise, he did. I guess everything happened for a reason, because I was happy that she asked to stay with me; Hakim was trying hard, as hell, to get back in with my sister, so I could understand why Hope didn't want to be there.

I strolled in the other bathroom to check on her, and I could hear her crying. When I opened the door, her eyes were red and puffy. She tried to wipe her face, but it was too late. I sat on the toilet to smoke a blunt, and shockingly, she asked to smoke.

"I didn't know you smoked, girl."

"Yea, well there's a lot of things you don't know about me."

"Oh, yea. Well, tell me."

We sat there talking for about an hour, before she kicked me out, so she could wash up. I told her it was too late, and that I had already saw her ass naked, but she still made me leave. I turned the TV on in my room and got comfortable. She came in my room, wearing a wife beater and some basketball shorts that I gave her. They were falling down off her, but she climbed into bed, got under the covers, snuggled up under me, and went to sleep.

I couldn't believe that the woman I loved was in my bed asleep. I just watched her sleep, peacefully, before I followed suit. I woke up and saw that she was gone, so I assumed that she went into the other room. My phone started ringing, and it was my mom asking if I would pick her a ham up for Sunday's dinner. There was a knock on my bedroom door, and then, she slid the door open.

"Word. You made a nigga breakfast?" I grinned and licked my lips at all the food she cooked. There were eggs, bacon, potatoes, grits, pancakes and toast.

"That's the least I could do since you let me crash here and listened to me talk about my problems."

"You got that. Do you want me to drop you off when I leave?"

"Yea. Paige is at work, now, so I won't get the third degree until later."

"What are you going to do for the rest of the day?"

"I don't know. Probably unpack and stay in the house. What about you?"

"Hit the streets and bullshit."

We talked some more before we were dressed and out the door. I parked in front of my sister's house. She reached for the handle, and I told her that if she didn't want to stay there that night, the other bedroom was hers, and you can imagine how happy a nigga was later when she took me up on that offer.

I dropped the key off to her and told her that I probably wouldn't be in until late, but I had another key. She stayed with me the whole week, kicking it with me like when we were young.

One night, I got to my house a little after two. I went to get something to drink out the fridge, when I saw a note on the counter.

"Hey, I left you some spaghetti in the fridge. There's also some garlic bread if you want some. Sorry, I was hungry. I left ten dollars to pay for what I used." I laughed and heated up the food.

I locked up, turned the lights off, and went to jump in the shower. When I opened my bedroom door, Hope was laid out on my bed with the TV on. I smiled to myself, because this is what I always wanted, but I wasn't not a rebound nigga, either.

After my shower, I put on some basketball shorts, grabbed my blunt, and sat in the living room. I always smoked in the dark and reflected on the day's events. My eyes were closed when Hope sat down on my lap.

"Hope, what are you doing?" She took the blunt out my hand and took a few pulls before giving me a shotgun. I felt my man rising the longer she sat there. I tried lifting her up, but she didn't want to move.

"I want you to make love to me, E. Right here, right now."

I took the blunt out my mouth and just looked at her. Most niggas would've jumped at the chance, but I couldn't. I had too much respect for her, and I wasn't going to let that nigga cause her to do something she would regret.

"Hope, you don't want that. You're hurt about what happened, and I don't want you like that. Plus, if I make love to you; that's it. No one else can have this. I'm not used to sharing, and I'm not about to start."

She looked at me, put one of my fingers in her mouth, and sucked on it. My dick was now standing straight up. She placed my hand down by her pussy, so I could see how wet she was.

I pushed my forehead into hers, and said, "Are you sure you want to do this? I'm not playing when I say this will be mines when I enter you."

"Yes, Eric, I want this. I've wanted this since we went out for your 21st birthday. I know exactly what I'm doing." I had to smile, because she was checking for me and never said a word. I reached behind her and put the blunt out in the ashtray.

We started kissing, as I raised the wifebeater over her head. Her breast popped out, and I made love to both of them, pushing them together flickering back and forth. She pushed my head closer into her and placed soft kisses on my neck. She stood up, took her panties off, pulled my man out, and guided herself down, slowly. We both moaned out in pure pleasure. She went up and down, grinding her hips in a circular motion.

She felt so good that I had to hold myself back from cumming already. I turned her around, spread her ass cheeks, and slid my tongue in her ass, then her pussy. I was so deep in that pussy that you would've thought I was trying to get inside. Her legs started shaking, and the massive amount of juices coming out let me know I did my job. She fell back on the couch, but I didn't stop. I pushed her legs back, wrapped my lips on her clit, and gave her another orgasm. She tried to close her legs, but I kept them open and made her cum a few more times.

I picked her up and carried her to my room. Once I placed her on the bed, I just stared for a few seconds and admired how pretty she was. I opened her legs and entered her again. She felt so good, as she allowed her pussy muscles to clutch my dick.

"Eric, this is better than I imagined. It feels so good. I'm about to cum, again."

"Oh, yea? Tell me it's my pussy first." I said, giving her slow stokes.

"Fuck, Eric, it's yours. Oh, my god; it's yours. Here I cummmm…. I let her catch her breath and turned her over. I guided my dick inside and continued making love to her. The skin smacking and wet noises from our sex was all you heard.

"Hope, I'm cummming baby…"

"Me, too, Eric! Don't stop. Fuuuuccckkk…" We both collapsed on the bed. After we got it together, she laid under my arm.

"Now what, Eric?"

"Nothing, I'm about to finish making love to you for the rest of the night." I told her, and we did just that. We both satisfied each other in ways we didn't even know was possible. We sexed each other down so much that when Sunday came neither one of us wanted to go to my mom's.

"Hope, we don't have to tell anyone, right now, if you don't want to. But, just know, I don't expect you to fuck nobody else, either."

"Eric, please. I don't care who knows. I never thought making love could be so good. But, just so you know, I don't expect you to fuck no one else, either."

"Hope, I've waited a long time for you, and if this is something we're going to pursue, I'm not losing you. Now, get up so we can go eat." I said, kissing her forehead.

She tried to go another round, but I stopped her. I knew that if we did, we would never leave the house, and I didn't want to hear my mom's mouth. I sent my sister a message to see where she was. When she sent a message back saying she was at my mom's, I dropped Hope off at her house, so we could drive in separate cars. I didn't pull up to my mom's house until 5:30, because I got caught up, but when I did, I saw Hakim and Ez on the porch talking. I didn't know what Ezrah was doing there, but fuck it.

Paige

I felt so bad for Hope, because I knew exactly what she was going through; the only difference was that he was having a baby on her. I sent Hakim a message to come over as soon as we got there and saw them fucking. I knew that that shit was going to get out of hand, quickly, because Ez was the same way over Hope that Hakim was over me. He wasn't going to let her go that easy; no matter what he told Ashley. He cheated, but he still thought Hope was his soul mate.

Hope wanted some time to herself, so I dropped her off at the bar, and that was last Monday. I hadn't seen that bitch since. She sent me a few text messages saying that she was okay and not to worry, but something was up.

Hakim and I had just got to my mom's house and Ez pulled up behind us.

"Hakim, I don't know if this is a good idea. They haven't seen each other since that day."

"Don't worry. Aint nothing going to happen. He won't disrespect your mom's house. Just as he said that, Hope parked across the street, came to give me a hug, and we walked in. She even said hello to Ez, which was shocking. She and I went in my old room, I locked the door, and told her ass to spill it.

"Ok, Paige. I'm not telling you who he is, but just know, he's special."

"Ok, you can tell me who he is later. What's up? Where the hell have you been?"

"The night I went to the bar, I ran into an old friend. I asked him to drop me off at your house, but Hakim was there, and I knew y'all asses was fucking, so I didn't want to hear that shit. We went to his house, and he listened to me talk about that dumb ass nigga outside. He wiped my eyes when I cried and didn't even touch me when I laid under him in his bed. Yes, his bed.

The next few days, he was out all day and I was be asleep when he came in. But one night, I stayed up watching some scary movie and couldn't sleep. When he came in, he got in the shower and went to smoke in the living room. I smelled it and stepped in the room with him. I don't know what came over me but I sat on his lap."

"Bitch, what? Did you fuck him?" She put her head down, laughing.

"Girl, yes, and I must say that that shit was the fucking bomb. That nigga showed me the true meaning of what it's like to have someone make love to you. Don't get it twisted; we had a lot of rough sex, too. Our bodies were so in sync with one another; it felt like we were supposed to have been together."

"Dammmmm, that nigga got you sprung already. So, now what?"

"We are a couple. but we haven't told anyone yet. Before you say anything, I know Ez and I just broke up, but to be honest with you, it's been over. We only had sex once last month, and shit hasn't been right for some time now."

"Ok, but what do you think he's going to do when he finds out you're with someone else?"

"Oh, I'm not worried about that. I have a trick for his ass today. You think I spoke because I wanted to? Hell no. Just wait for the surprise, boo." I noticed her phone vibrating, and when she looked at her phone, a huge smile crept across her face. I assumed that it was that new dude. I couldn't wait to meet who had her that happy. We walked down the steps, and my brother, Eric, walked in giving me and Hope a hug before going to the back with my dad.

"Paige, come here for a minute, please?" My mom called from the kitchen.

"Yes, mom." I saw Hope sitting at the table texting away on her phone.

"Are you and Hakim back together? And, don't play stupid. I know y'all broke up after the accident."

"Ma, how did you know?"

"Girl, aint no man going to punch a hole in the wall and break his hand for nothing." I couldn't do anything but laugh.

I told her that I would be right back, because my dad gestured for me to come see him. I stepped outside, and Eric was on his phone, texting away, with a big ass cheese on his face.

"What the hell? Is everybody in the mood to be texting instead of talking today? You out here going at it, Hope in there doing the same thing."

I looked at his face change, then I looked in the house, and Hope was looking at me. I glanced back at my brother and shook those thoughts out my head. She would never mess with my brother.

"Hey, dad. What's up?" We took a walk and sat on the bench.

"Baby girl, you know I'm happy about you being pregnant, but do you think it's a good thing to bring a baby in this world right now with y'all fighting."

"Dad, we're in a good space right now. We may not be together, but we have a mutual respect for one another. He's still my baby's daddy, so he's going to be around."

"Ok, if that's what you want. Do you love him?" I put my head on his shoulder before I answered.

"Yes. I'm in love with him, but daddy, you know I'm not stupid, either. I won't allow him to walk all over me, and I think he realizes that now. He's trying to get it right, but I'm making him suffer."

"That's my girl. Make him work for you. Don't let him off easy." My dad got up and went in the kitchen with my mom.

"Come sit with me, Eric." He put his phone in the case on his hip and sat next to me. I put my legs on his and stared at him.

"Eric, you know I love you right. You're my favorite brother. Do you have anything you want to tell me?" I saw him trying to avoid my stare. I knew he was hiding something; I just didn't know what it was.

"Yes, Paige, and you are my favorite sister. I'm not hiding anything from you. Just know that when it's time for things to come to surface, they will. Come on, let's go eat; you're not going to starve my niece or nephew." He said, helping me up. Everyone was seated at the table, when I noticed that Hakim saved me a seat next to him.

"How do you know I want to sit by you?" He kissed my lips and laughed. My dad said the grace and everybody started filling their plates up."

“Hope, why aren’t you sitting next to Ezrah?”Just as she said that, Ez looked up and the doorbell rang. I’ll get it, Ma.”

We all looked around like what the hell was going on; I thought Ezrah was going to choke when he saw Ashley come in. I squeezed Hakim’s leg, and he continued eating like nothing happened.

“Ma, this is Ashley. Ashley, this is my second mother, dad, and the introductions continued. Oh, and you know Ezrah. Here, I saved you a seat right next to him.”

“Hope, what is going on?” My mom asked. My dad just shook his head, laughing.

“Ma, you just asked me why I didn’t sit next to Ezrah. I was saving a seat for his new girlfriend, oh my bad, his baby momma.” Ezrah was so mad you could see the steam coming out his ears, as Ashley grabbed his hand.

“Ezrah, is this true?” He didn’t get a chance to answer before Ashley cut in.

“Yes. I am four months, and Ezrah and I are so excited. We go Tuesday to see what we’re having. We’ve been setting up the baby's room so that, when I get bigger, everything's already done."

"Oh, that's great. So, you guys moved in together, yet?" Hope asked, being smart.

"No, Hope. You guys just broke up; what was that last Monday. Yea; we've been out house hunting since." I could see Hope shaking her head, grinning. I knew that this was about to get ten times worse.

Ezrah

It had been almost a week since I had talked to Hope. I went to her job, and they said that she took a leave of absence until further notice. She blocked my number from her phone, and I even stayed at Paige's house for two days to wait for her to come, and she never did. Ashley had me house shopping with her and decorating a nursery in her house, until we got a bigger one. I had to get Hope back, but I had to figure out how to keep both of them.

I went to Paige's mom's for Sunday dinner, which I knew she never missed. She got out the car, and was wearing some black, fitted jeans, a sweater that came to her stomach, and some thigh boots. She looked beautiful and even spoke when she walked on the porch. When her and Paige came downstairs, I called her outside.

"Hope, can I talk to you for a minute." She came out on the porch and sat in one of the chairs.

"What's up, Ezrah?"

"Oh, I'm Ezrah, now? Ok, you got that?"

“Yes, you’re not my man, anymore. There’s no need for nicknames, anymore.” Her phone went off, and when she looked down, smiling, I wanted to snatch that phone out her hand to see who was making her smile. I was so jealous, because that used to be me.

“Ezrah, are you going to stare at me, or are you going to tell me why you asked me to come out here?”

“I’m sorry, Hope.”

“Ok, is that all? Matter of fact, just tell me why you did it?”

“I don’t know, Hope. You gave me everything I needed, plus some. I guess I was just thinking with my dick and didn’t believe I would get caught. The baby was unexpected, though.”

“Oh, so I’m supposed to be relieved that that was an accident? Nigga, you knew what it was when you kept screwing her without a condom and don’t come to me with that it was only one time.” Hope had me stuck. I thought that I could say that I was sorry and she would take me back, but her ass wasn't having it. The entire time she stayed texting someone on her phone.

"Look, Ezrah. I'll admit that I was so hurt. I didn't think you would do some shit like that to me, but I was wrong. All I have ever asked you for was honesty and to love me, and you couldn't do that. Let's be honest, over the last couple of months, things have changed, and I guess I know why now. We had sex once in the last three weeks, and we used to have sex once or twice a day. You thought with your dick and let that woman come in and destroy what we had built. It's obvious that me being a little older than you was too much. I wanted someone faithful to love me as his one and only, and you failed, so if there's nothing else to say, have a good life." She said and walked back in the house. I couldn't do anything but sit there.

What really took the cake was her inviting Ashley over for dinner. I almost choked on my food when she came in. Then, Ashley started running off at the mouth about me buying her a house, and I knew, right then, that Hope was never coming back. I knew that shit was about to hit the fan, especially, when the doorbell rang, again, and Noel walked in.

“Hi everyone. Noel said.

“Hey, Noel. Have a seat.” Paige said, pointing to one of the chairs.” She just smiled and took a seat on the other side of Hakim.

“Mom and dad, I don’t want you to think I’m being disrespectful, but this was the only time that I could get everyone together. I need all of the bullshit out on the table, so that we can move on.”

“Paige, I’m about to leave. I don’t want to deal with this.” I told her.

“No, Ezrah, you sit right there. That’s what’s wrong with everyone. When shit hit the fan, someone is always trying to run, so we’re going to sit here until it’s settled. Ma, you and dad don’t have to stay.”

“Hell no! I want to see how this plays out myself.” Paige’s mom said, while her dad took his plate and went to his room.

Ok, Ezrah, what you did to Hope was foul as hell. Just as foul as what Hakim did to me. Now I get it, you two were dealing with these chicks before we came around, but once you laid down with us, that was supposed to stop. What I don't understand is, if y'all are out there doing you, why can't you let us go?"

"Hope is my soul mate. I don't want to leave her alone. Ashley was just someone I was screwing, and now, she's pregnant; I won't leave my kid."

"Hope, do you want to be with Ezrah?" When she shook her head no, I got so mad, I slammed my fist down on the table.

"Hope, stop acting like a baby. You and Ashley are going to get along, and you and I are going to work this out." Ashley was grinning, but Hope was getting ready to smack the shit out of her, so my brother stood in between the two of them.

I thought we were done until she asked Noel when was the last time her and Hakim were together. She said the night of the party and pulled her phone out to let Paige see some text messages between them two over the last few days. Paige smacked the shit out of him, and he just sat there.

"I'm telling you, right now, Paige. Whenever Hakim calls I'm going to come running. If he wants to have sex or even wants me to go down on him, I'm there. We got time in, and even though you're pregnant, he's still going to fuck with me. You should know that; look what happened at the BBQ." She was so confident in her words. Hakim stood up, took Noel's hand, and left. A few minutes later, he walked back in, without Noel, and sat right back down next to Paige.

"Hakim, I'm done. I told you to keep it one hundred with me, and instead, you protected whatever you shared with her. I'll call you when I have the baby. I don't even think I can stomach you while I'm in the delivery room."

"Paige, I'm not going anywhere." He said and leaned back in his chair.

"Hakim, there's a thin line between me and you. And, you snapped it this last time with you and Noel's shit. I'm tired of this back and forth with y'all. Every time I think we're in a good space, somehow, she's there to ruin it. This is all happening, because you can't say no to her."

"Please, leave me alone. I'm asking you, nicely. I'm telling you in front of everyone that I don't want to be with you, anymore." She said, with tears running down her face.

"Paige, we are never going to be over. You're mad right now, and I get it, but you're not leaving me, so get that out of your head."

She gave her mom a kiss and left. I felt like we were on the movie "Why Did I Get Married" when they were sitting at the table and all the secrets came pouring out.

"Ok, then. I'm leaving with my sister. I'll see you later, baby." Hope said and kissed Eric. I jumped out my chair, trying to get to him. He took his chain and his shirt off, and challenged me in the front yard. Hakim stood in between us.

"Really, E? You grimy like that?"

"Nah, nigga. You fucked up, and she chose me. I didn't go out looking for her; she found me. Me and you ain't cool like that. We only speak on the strength of Hakim and the girls, so if you on some fighting shit, let's go."

"He's right, Ez, man. Y'all not friends, and you only hung together a few times, because of me. You can't be mad at this man over that. But look, you're my cousin, and he my man, so I don't want either one of y'all fighting."

"You taking his side, Hakim?"

"I'm not taking anybody's side. Shit, I have my own shit to deal with, as you can see. But, I'm not about to sit here and let y'all fight. Ez that was Hope's decision, and be honest, you pushed her right into the arms of the next man, so how can you be mad?"

"And, E, you're my boy, and my girl's brother. Well, ex until I figure that out. You and Ez need to peace that shit up and move on."

"I'm good. That's your cousin on his bullshit." He said, putting his stuff back on. I just shook my head, gave him that man hug, and apologized.

"You're right, my bad. We cool, and I respect that you were ready to fight for her. That let's me know that she picked a good man. I'm out. Let's go, Ashley." That day was a disaster. So much for getting Hope back now.

Hakim

"Come on, Paige, I'm hungry as hell." I yelled in the backroom, as I rolled up. She came walking out in some jeans, a sweater, and some ankle boots. She was a little over three months now, so her stomach had a little poke to it. She stood in front of me and pulled her sweater up.

"Do you see my belly growing? I'm so excited, babe." She was glowing, and the sparkle in her eye had me excited to be in her life.

"I see." I kissed her stomach, and got up to leave. I knew if we stayed any longer we would be in the bedroom for the rest of the day.

When we got to her mom's, Hope pulled up across the street. She spoke to all of us, as Paige grabbed her in the house to talk I guess. Everyone was sitting at the table, when Ashley walked in, then Noel, came in not too much later. I couldn't believe what the hell was going on right in front of me. Noel's dumb ass told Paige we slept together after the party and showed her the damn messages we sent each other.

I didn't know why I kept dealing with Noel. I loved her, but I was not in love with her; I just couldn't leave her alone, either. Anyway, after she ran her mouth, I walked her to her car.

"Noel, why can't you just keep your mouth shut? Now, we agreed that you would be my side chick, but now, you in here running off telling her everything."

"I don't want to be your side chick, Hakim. I want to be your main one. I'm the one that's been holding you down. Every time you fuck up; she leaves, but I'm the one that's still here. Yet, you keep going back to her. What is it? Is her pussy that good?"

"Noel, I would never discuss anything concerning Paige with you, so don't ever ask. As far as why I keep going back, she is having my baby. I'm not letting my baby grow up in two different households."

"Hakim, I'm supposed to be the one having your baby, not her." She started crying.

I closed the door and told her that I would be by later. I strolled back in the house, and Paige kept saying that she was leaving me, but I wasn't worried about that shit. After I broke the shit up with my cousin and her brother, I went outside and her and Hope were just getting in the car. I guess Hope was waiting for Eric, because when he came out, she hugged him and those fools acted like they were about to fuck on the front lawn.

"Hope, can we go please? You can see him later." I heard Paige yelling out the car.

"Paige, get out the car." I loved that she was a classy woman. She would never let her temper bring her out of character for others to see.

"Hakim, I'm done this time. You don't have to worry about me sleeping with no one else, because I'm not like that. You don't respect me or the relationship we had. And, to think that I was going to tell you tonight that we could be together, but once again, you chose her."

"I didn't choose her."

"Please stop. I'm so tired of your pathetic ass lies and excuses on why you are still dealing with her. But, she was right when she said that she is the one with your heart. She has time in, and all I have is this baby in my stomach and heartache. I think it's best for you not to contact me from here on out. If I need you, I will hit you up."

"Paige, I don't care who I'm with. You will always come first. I don't want anyone but you. Why can't you see that?"

"Uhhh, I can't see it, because when I turn my back for one second, you're back with her. Why are you making this harder than it has to be?"

"I don't want you with anyone else."

"Hakim, who am I going to be with pregnant?"

"Paige, you are everything to me. Why can't you see that?"

"So, you're telling me that if I tell you to cut Noel completely off, you can do it?"

"Yes, I'll do anything to keep you in my life."

"Ok, tomorrow, we'll have her meet at your mom's house, and you can tell her then." She said. I tried to kiss her, but she turned her head.

"You got that. I'll see you, tomorrow."

Whew! That was a close one. Now, I had to deal with that bitch. I was going to leave her alone, for real, this time. She was causing too much havoc in my life. I stopped by the liquor store, picked up some Henney, and a few wraps for my blunts. I checked in with all my soldiers and headed to my mom's house for the night. I sent Paige a message.

Me: *I miss you. Can I come over?*

Paige: *I miss you, too. Not tonight. Where are you?*

Me: *I'm staying at my mom's since I can't be with you.*

Paige: *Ok, be safe. I'll see you tomorrow.*

I'm sitting in my truck when this chick rolls up. *Fuck, I forgot to call her ass.* I get out the truck and walked to her car. I didn't want her nowhere in my shit, because I didn't need no chick's perfume in there.

"Pull into the driveway. I can't sit on the street smoking in the car." She pulled up, and I got in. I lit my blunt, put my head back, and closed my eyes. Neither one of us spoke. After a few more pulls, I finally said something.

"Noel, I think we really need to end this."

"Oh, we back on this shit again. Nigga please. I thought about what you said. I will play the side chick role. I swear, you better not play me out or let her get out of pocket with me. The only reason I've considered this is because I love you, and if that's the only way for me to be with you, then I will." I blew smoke out and thought about what she said.

"Nah, I think I'm going try and work it out with Paige. I don't want to keep taking her through this shit with you. She never gave me a reason to treat her like that, yet, I'm breaking her heart every chance I get, because of you."

"But, what about me? You broke my heart plenty of times, and I stayed."

"You're right, Noel, but all of this running back and forth is confusing you and her. I shouldn't be treating you like that, either, and I'm sorry. This time, I'm serious when I say it's over between us. Noel, you deserve better than me." She started tearing up, but I couldn't feel bad for her, because she didn't give a fuck about nobody but herself.

"Ok, Hakim, if that's what you want. Just know that I'm not going to be here this time for you to come running back." She leaned over and kissed me. She hopped on my lap, and instead of stopping her, I allowed her to keep going. She pulled her skirt up and didn't have no panties on, which let me know she came for this. Fuck it; I'll give her one for the road.

She unbuckled my pants, and went for a ride.

"Fuck, Noel. This is the last time, I swear. I said, guiding her hips back and forth.

"Ok, baby, just fuck me. Shit, it feels good." I could feel her nut coming down my pole spilling on my clothes.

"Get in the back." We jumped out, and I entered her from behind and fucked her the way she liked it.

"Shit, I'm about to cum, Noel."

"Cum in me, daddy." I was not about to let my seeds off in her.

"I want you to suck it." She turned around and sucked the life out of me. She wiped her mouth with the back of her hand, then, I pulled her up, and we both sat back in the car. When I looked up, Paige and Hope were right there shaking their heads. I couldn't believe I got busted, again. I knew that

Paige was never come back after this.

Paige

The Sunday dinner was a complete mess. Ashley showed up, and then, Noel told me that her and Hakim had sex. She even showed me all the text messages between them. The one I remembered the most was when he told her that if she kept her mouth shut, he would keep giving her the dick. I knew that he was still fucking with her; that's why when he told me he was at his mom's, I was going to pop up. He wouldn't leave me alone, so if I caught his ass out there, again, maybe he'll know. The last time he was caught, he left me alone. I hate to say it, but I hoped I caught him so that he could let me move on.

Hope and my brother ended up staying at my house, because she didn't want to leave me after what happened at my mom's. But, they wanted to be together, so here they are. We were watching a moving when Hakim asked to come over a little after eleven. I told him no, because I knew that he thought I was in bed. Eric was in the extra bedroom, watching ESPN, when Hope and I snuck out.

"Girl, what are you going to do if you catch him?"

"Nothing really, Hope. I just want him to see me like you did with Ez. I don't want him to deny shit." When we pulled up, I had Hope turn the lights off in her car.

Noel pulled up, and he had her pull in the driveway. We watched him get in her car, and then, smoke came out the window. A few minutes later, you could see through the back window that they were kissing, and she jumped in his lap. Once the car started rocking, I knew what it was. Not too long after, they crawled in the back seat, and the car rocked some more.

"Are you okay?" Hope asked, as the tears flowed down my face.

"Yup, I'm good. Grab your phone; I want to record this shit. I don't want him to say I was seeing things."

We walked to the front of her car and they were so into it that they didn't even know we were standing there. When I saw her come up from, I guess, sucking his dick; Hope and I stood there with our arms folded, and when his eyes opened, the look on his face was priceless.

I opened the door, and said, “I hope you enjoyed yourselves.” I wiped the tears from my eyes and marched back to Hope’s car. He came running behind me buttoning up his pants, and she stood there with a smirk on her face.

“Paige, let me whoop that bitch’s ass, please?”

“Nah, Hope, because then, it would look like I was mad that he fucked her, and I’m not. I’m hurt, but not mad.”

“Hakim, don’t say shit to me. I came to surprise you and looks like the surprise was on me, again.”

“Paige, I swear I told her it was over.”

“Oh, you did. How did she take it? Oh, I’m sorry. She took it well in the front and back seat.” I could see the way his face turned up.

“Yea, I saw when she got here, and we been sitting here waiting for you to finish. It sounds crazy, but I’m happy you slept with her.”

“What the fuck you mean by that?”

“It means just what I said. I know you don’t still believe we can be together after this.”

"Paige, you should just leave him alone. He's not going to stop fucking me. Even if he did, I'm still going to be his side chick. I showed you the messages, so why do you keep taking him back?"

"You're right. I'm stupid to think he could love me. So, I want you two to be happy together. Hakim, this is where you want to be, so I hope that you can respect my decision and back off."

"We are having a baby. I'm going to always be in your life."

"Oh, I didn't tell you. I am making an appointment in the morning to terminate the pregnancy. I can't bring a baby into the world like this. Hakim this shit right here is toxic and not healthy for me?" I saw the hurt wash across his face when I said that, and I didn't care, because all he was been doing was hurting me.

"Paige, it's too late to get rid of the baby, so stop talking crazy."

"I have all the way up to 14 weeks, and I'm only 12 ½ right now. So, don't think I haven't done my research about it."

"Don't worry, baby, you and I are going to have a bunch of babies. You don't need her. If she wants to get rid of it, let her." Noel said. I thought he was going to kill her when she said that. He grabbed her by the throat and threw her ass on the ground.

"Now, Hakim, you don't have to do that to her. She's only speaking the truth, and by the way you two are fucking, I'm sure she'll be expecting soon. We had a good time together. But, for you that's all it was. Now, accept this shit, and stay the fuck out of my life." I yelled at him. I sat down in the car, and he wouldn't let me shut the door.

"What the fuck, Hakim? Let the door go."

He bent down in front of me and said, "Paige, please don't abort my baby."

"Hakim, I'm done with you, and if I keep the baby, then I will have to deal with you for eighteen years, so please respect my decision."

"Paige, I have never put my hands on you, but I swear to God, if you get an abortion, I will fucking kill you." He said, through gritted teeth. The way he said it sent chills down my spine. He had me scared, as hell, but I wouldn't show it.

"Whatever, Hakim. You aren't doing shit. Go threaten her with that shit."

"Paige, if you don't want me no more, okay, but my baby better stay in your stomach for six more months. I'm not going to say it again. Get rid of the baby, and you will be looking over your shoulder for the rest of your life, which will be cut short when I find you."

"Bye, Hakim." He finally let me shut the door. Hope pulled off, and we drove back to my house.

"Bitch, are you really getting an abortion?"

"Hell no. I told his ass that, so that he could leave me the fuck alone. I don't get it Hope. I caught him, again, thinking that would make him leave, and he still won't leave me alone."

"Girl, you must have that bomb ass pussy."

"I thought that, at first, but I don't feel like I do if he still fucking around."

"Paige, men could have the best woman at home. I mean, she'll cook, clean, take it in the ass, toss his salad, have threesomes, you name it, and he will still cheat. It's what the fuck they do. Now, I'm not sure why he keeps running back to her, but I doubt if it's good pussy, because he treats her like shit. Maybe, he is just comfortable with her." We got back to the house, and Eric was knocked out in Hope's room.

"All right, girl. I need to lay up under my man." She said and closed her door.

I took a shower, and laid on my couch, watching Snapped. I was watching an episode of a woman who walked in on her husband cheating, and she killed both of them. I looked at the clock, and it was after midnight. I heard a knock at the door, and I knew who it was.

"What Hakim?" I didn't even look at him when I opened the door.

"Come outside. I want to talk to you?" I opened the screen door and sat on the top step. He sat in front of me, and when I tried to move, he leaned back in between my legs.

"Paige, I don't know why I keep fucking up. All I know is I'm breaking your heart. Every time I see you cry, my heart hurts."

"Hakim, if you know you're hurting me, then let me go? Why keep creeping back in my life and repeating the same shit?"

"I don't want you with anyone else. You caught me twice already having sex with Noel, and I don't know how you're dealing with it, because if I caught you with another man, I'm killing both of y'all. I can't see any other man giving you pleasure and making your body do what I can."

"Hakim, this has gotten so bad. Why couldn't we just stay the way we were at the beginning, so that we wouldn't have these problems?"

"I was being selfish. I knew if we kept it like that, then, you would be free to be with someone else, and I couldn't take it."

"Hakim, we will always be friends, but we can't be in a relationship. I will always love you, but please just let me go."

I stood up to go back in the house, but he grabbed my arm and turned me to face him.

"You love me?" He asked.

"Yes, Hakim, I do. I'm in love with you; that's why it's killing me that you couldn't keep your dick in your pants. We could've been so good together." I said, now letting my own tears fall.

"Why didn't you tell me?"

"It wouldn't have made a difference. Not only that, I shouldn't have had to tell you for you to not sleep with someone else."

He lifted my chin and kissed me. He picked me up with our tongues still wrestling and brought me in the house. He locked the door and followed me to my bedroom. I picked up my phone and turned it on Pandora's, so Hope and my brother couldn't hear me. I let him make love to me all night. We both cried and apologized, but I knew that that still wasn't right.

I woke up the next day before him, got dressed, kissed his lips, left, and never went back.

Kamal

When Paige called me the other day to ask if she could stay with me, at first, I was hesitant. The last time that she asked, she never came. She pulled up around four in the morning, and instead, of going back to sleep, I just stayed up watching her sleep. I missed the hell out of that woman, but I was now dealing with someone else. I still couldn't allow myself to leave Paige stranded when she needed me. She could've gone to a hotel, or her parent's house, but she didn't.

I left my house a little after eight so that I could get to work on time. I was in the middle of a meeting when my phone started vibrating.

Paige: *Good morning, well, good afternoon. I just wanted to say thank you for allowing me to stay with you. I'm not going to crowd your space; I just needed to get away.*

Me: *It's ok. You can stay as long as you like.*

Paige: *Thanks Kamal*

Me: *Have a good day at work.*

Paige: *You too*

After work, I stopped by Janine's house. Janine is the new woman in my life, and I must say that every time I see her, she makes me smile. She was brown-skinned, maybe 5'2, short hair, and a beautiful personality. She reminded me of a shorter version of Sanaa Lathan. She was a high school teacher and the cheerleading coach. I pulled in her driveway at the same time she did.

"Hey, Baby. How was your day?

"It was good, but I thought about you most of the time." I told her.

"Oh, yea. So, who were you thinking about the rest of the time?"

"Well, if you must know. I was thinking about her." I said, pointing to her love box.

She took my hand and guided me in the house. We kissed each other, hungrily, stripping one another of our clothes. I picked her up and let her go for a ride. Janine and I had sex four to five times a week and sometimes more. The first time we had sex, I was nervous, because I wasn't sure what she liked, and I didn't really know anything outside of Paige's and my sex life. But, she took her time and taught me what she liked, and in return, she showed me a lot of new things.

After we finished, I pulled her close to me. "Janine, I have to talk to you." She scooted under me and looked up.

"What's up, baby?" I told her about Paige coming over a few days ago, and to my surprise, she wasn't upset.

"Ok, so are you trying to get back with her?" I lifted her face, so that she could look in my eyes.

"No, Janine. I'm more than happy with you."

"Good. How long is she staying?" She asked, now jumping in the shower.

"I don't know. I think something is going on with her and that young dude she's messing with."

After she came out and got dressed, we went into the kitchen to finish talking, and my phone started vibrating. When I looked, it was Paige.

Paige: *Hey, I hope you don't mind, I invited Hope over for dinner."*

Me: *No, that's fine. I probably won't be back tonight. I'm with Janine.*

Paige: *Oh, bring her over, I would love to meet her.*

Me: *Ok, let me ask her.*

"Janine, Paige just sent me a message saying she cooked dinner; she wanted me to invite you. Do you want to go?"

"Sure, why not. I want to meet the woman that let you go and sent you into my life."

Me: *We'll be there in a few.*

Paige: *Ok great.*

I jumped in the shower and threw some jeans and a t-shirt on that I had over Janine's house. We pulled up, and I saw Hope getting out of Eric's truck, but not before seeing them kiss. I just shook my head, because all those years around of being friends, I guess they finally got together. I waved to both of them, opened Janine's car door, and headed inside.

"Paige, this is Janine. Janine, this is Paige." I could see Hope walking through the door out the side of my eye.

"Hi, Janine. It's really nice to meet you. I hope you like London broil. I made that with potatoes, string beans, and a salad."

"Yes, I do, and thanks for the invite. You must be Hope."

"Yes, I am. Hi, Janine."

We all sat at the table talking about how we met and what everybody had going on in our lives. Janine seemed to relax after the introduction, and that was good, because I wanted them to get along. Paige's phone was going off, and I could see that her entire demeanor changed.

"Hope, call Eric please, and tell him to get over here, quick." We all looked at Paige trying to figure out what was going on. Just then, someone was banging on the door. Hope picked her phone up to make the call while I went to get the door.

“Yo’, is Paige here?” I looked him up and down then back to Paige.

“What do you want, Hakim?” I thought Janine was going to fall out the chair when I said his name. I stepped out of the way, so that he could come in. I lived in a quiet neighborhood, and I didn’t want people in my business.

“Hey, Janine.” He said, walking past her to get to Paige.

“Wait, what. How do you know, Janine?” Paige asked him.

“Oh, that’s Noel’s sister.” The face Paige made was out of pure disgust.

“Hakim, you can’t just barge in somebody’s house demanding to see me.” He scoffed up a laugh and kept talking.

“Paige, I’m tired of playing these games with you. Let’s go. I’m tired of coming home, and you’re not there.”

“Home?! Nigga we don’t live together. And, you can sleep up under Noel, so don’t give me that.” I could see that Janine was uncomfortable.

"Paige, I don't want her. I keep telling you that. Let's work this out." There was another knock at the door, but Hope went to answer it.

"Hey, Eric. Can you take him with you, please? I don't know how he found me, but it's best that he leaves."

"Paige, I'm not leaving with out you. Eric, man, I'm not going without her." Everybody just stood there, silently, because no one wanted to set him off. Paige must've known he wasn't budging, so she just agreed.

"Ok, Hakim, damn. I'll be at my house in a few. Let me clean up."

"Come on, man." Eric said, pushing him out the door.

"Paige, don't make me come back to get you. I'll be at the house in an hour." He said, walking out.

"So, you're the infamous Paige?" Janine said, making us all look.

"What do you mean by that?" Hope barked at her. Paige put the dishrag down and stood in the kitchen to hear what she had to say.

"I don't mean anything by that. I know you're the Paige he used to be married to, but I didn't know you were the one my sister was talking about." I sat down to listen to Janine, and I must say that her sister was crazy as hell. No wonder she didn't fuck with her like that.

Hakim

"Noel, you have to go, now, and don't come back. This shit with you is throwing me off my square, and I can't have that."

"Hakim, don't yell at me. This is your fault, because you don't have to fuck me. You want me to feel bad, because she keep catching us. Well, I don't. I hope that this time she really leaves you, then maybe we can be together."

"That's just it, Noel. I'm not going to let her leave me. She is the best thing that has happened in my life. I keep fucking up, because I'm allowing you to make me feel guilty for shit that happened years ago. It wasn't anybody's fault, and I know, now, that we both have to move on from that."

I didn't even give her time to speak, before I went into my mom's house to shower. I'm not going to front, I shed some tears in the shower for Paige. I knew that I was in love with her, but I couldn't get past my own selfishness to love her right. I threw some sweats and t-shirt on, because I had to see Paige to explain shit to her.

I got to her house, and she was still up. We sat outside and talked when, out of nowhere, she told me she loved me. A nigga was happy, as hell, but I still couldn't find the words to tell her the words back. It wasn't that I didn't love her; I was just scared. She let me make love to her all night. I woke up the next morning to find that she had left. There was a note on the nightstand.

Dear Hakim,

I can't do this, anymore. I am so in love with you that it's blinding me from seeing what type of person you really are. And, that is a selfish and arrogant man. I tried to love you in so many ways, but you couldn't handle it. I've always kept it one hundred with you, yet, you kept so many secrets from me. I promise that I won't abort the baby, because I can tell that you, at least, have some love in your heart for him or her. There's just no love in your heart for me. I will call you when I go into labor so you can witness the birth. All I ask is that you give me time to heal. Don't come looking for me and take care of yourself. I will always love you.

P.S.

Don't treat the next woman the way you did me. She doesn't deserve that. Stay safe.

Paige

Fuck that. I knocked on Hope's door. "Hope, where is Paige."

"Hakim, just let her be."

"I can't do that, Hope. Are you going to tell me where she is?"

"You know I'm not. Listen, I'll try and talk to her, but Hakim, she gave you so many chances, and you fucked up each time. What did you expect her to do?"

"I know, Hope, but I promise, I'll never hurt her, again. I just need to talk to her."

"Okay, I'll ask her to call you, but until then, you need to handle that Noel shit. If she did decide to take you back, that shit needs to be completely over."

"I deaded that shit last night after y'all left. If I have to get rid of Noel just for Paige to take me back, I will."

"Oh, my God, Hakim don't say that. If it's meant for you and her to be together you will be." Eric came out the room, shaking his head laughing.

"What you laughing at, bro?"

"Your ass. How you let my sister throw you off your square like that?"

"Whatever, nigga. I see this one is about to do the same to you if you're not careful." Hope smiled.

"Nah, for real, why do you want Paige back so bad?"

"Yo', E, I love the shit out of Paige. I just needed to get out of my own way."

"Listen, I don't like the shit you're putting my sister through, but she told me to stay out of her business a long time ago. I can see that you love her, but if you're not done fucking around with, not just Noel, but other bitches, then maybe you should let her be."

"Nah, hell no. Paige belongs with me. The faster she realizes that, the better."

"Hakim, you funny as hell. My sister must've threw it on your ass for you to be acting like this."

"Whatever, nigga. Let's hit these streets."

Three days went by, and I still hadn't heard from Paige. I spent the night at my mom's house every night, and each night, Noel came over begging for me to take her back.

"Ok, Hakim. She's not coming back this time. Can we try us again?" I just sat there listening to her go on and on about how good our life was going to be when we got back together. She tried to kiss me, and I moved back.

"Noel, I'm not doing this with you, again. This is over. I thought it was just me fucking up, but I see now you wanted me to. You don't want me to be happy with anyone but you. But, did you ever take the time out to think that, no matter how many times we fucked, I still never chose you over her?" I had her stuck, as she sat there trying to think about what I said.

“Alright, if this is what you want. Just remember that it’s not over until I say it is.”

“Go head with that shit, Noel.” I let her walk off the porch, and hopefully, out of my life. I sat there for a long time engaged in my thoughts until my mom came and took a seat next to me.

“Hakim, I’ve never seen you this obsessed over a woman. What is it about Paige?”

“Ma, it’s everything about her. She doesn’t take any of my shit, its the way she smiles,the way she smells, dresses, and I can’t front, she put it on a nigga.” I chuckled, thinking about how she had me weak with her head game the first time we made love.

“Ok, so if that’s true, why did you let Noel disrupt your relationship?”

“I don’t know. I think it’s because I knew that she would always have my back no matter how many times I cheated on her. Plus, that shit that we went through a few years ago. She still brings it up, and I think I allowed her to make me believe that it was my fault, so I felt I was supposed to always be there for her."

"Baby, you can't allow her to make you feel like that. If she was a real woman, she wouldn't have even expected you to. What happened could've and has happened to many other women. But, what you have to realize is that Paige caught you fucking her, not once, but twice, and still didn't react off of it. I think you're going to push her until she snaps, and then, what. Maybe, you should sit down and tell her the truth, and hopefully, she can take you back. But, you're not going to win her back, sitting on this porch smoking your life away."

"I know. I'm just trying to find the right time to go get her."

"Oh, so you know where she is?" I gave my mom this look like who do you think I am.

"Of course, I do. I still have Big John keeping an eye on her. After the accident, anytime she got in the car, I made sure that he's stuck to her bumper like white on rice. I don't ever want to see her laid up in the hospital like that again."

"Well, get some sleep, tonight, and go get your woman tomorrow. Her mom stopped by the other day."

"She did. I know she was mad about everything that took place."

"Actually, we had a good laugh over that. We went back and forth on what we would've done if that were us. She even had a few drinks with me." I gave my mom the side eye when she said that. "I'm serious. It was some wine, but we had a good time. She's waiting for you to win Paige back. She loves you for Paige, but you have to find your way back to make her forgive you. She didn't raise a dumb daughter, so believe me when I say, you're going to have to work hard. Don't lose her for the next man to step in and take her."

I gave my mom a hug and mentally prepared myself for the next day. I was going to win Paige back. The next day, I went to her ex husband's house. He opened the door, looking corny, as hell, but then, I saw Noel's sister, Janine. I didn't know why she was there, but hey I didn't care.

"Let's go, Paige." Of course, she put up a fight, until she finally gave in.

"Ok, Hakim. Damn, I'll be there, shortly." I took her hand and made her walk to the car with me.

"Paige, I want to tell you the truth about Noel and I."

"What you mean the truth?"

"It's not like I didn't tell you the truth. I just didn't tell you all of it. That's why I want you to come home. I want to lay all my cards on the table."

"Home? Again, with this. Nigga, you don't live with me." She said. I saw a smile creep across her face.

"I love you so much, Paige, and I can't take this back and forth. I want and need you in my life. Please say you'll come back to me."

"You love me, Hakim?" She asked, letting a few tears fall. I took my fingers, wiped them away, and kissed her passionately.

"I am in love with you, Paige. It took me a while to realize it, but I know now. I can't live without you."

"Baby, let me clean up, and get my stuff, but I promise I'm coming." We kissed some more before she turned to walk in.

"Damn, nigga, y'all getting on my nerves. Just fucking get married, already." Eric said.

"That's the plan." I said, jumping in my truck.

I got to Paige's house about two hours later, and saw that Noel's car was there. I thought I heard screaming, but I wasn't sure. When I walked in, Paige had her hands up, while Noel had the gun pressed to the back of her head. Hope walked in behind me.

"What the fuck are you doing, Noel?"

"Hakim, the only way we're going to be together is if I get rid of this bitch."

"Noel, stop. I'm never going to be with you, again. If you want to be mad at somebody, let it be me. She doesn't have anything to do with it." I said, walking closer to her. She started to lower the gun, when Paige took the chance to punch her in the face. I snatched Paige up, because she was pregnant, but we watched Hope beat the brakes off of her. When Hope finally got off her, Noel rolled over and pointed the gun. Paige pushed Hope out the way, and the gun went off.

"NOOOOOOOOOOOO!!!" Hope screamed.